MARIE KRYSINSKA

THE PATH OF AMOUR

TRANSLATED AND WITH AN INTRODUCTION BY

BRIAN STABLEFORD

THE PATH OF AMOUR

MARIE KRYSINSKA (1857-1908) was a Symbolist poet, novelist, and musician. She was born in Warsaw, Poland, and went to Paris at the age of sixteen to study musical composition at the Conservatoire. An important pioneer of *vers libre*, and rightly regarded as its inventor, she published three volumes of verse, *Rythmes pittoresques* (1890), *Joies errantes* (1894), and *Intermèdes, nouveaux rythmes pittoresques* (1903). She further published the short story collection *L'Amour chemine* (1892), and the novel *La Force du désir* (1905).

BRIAN STABLEFORD'S scholarly work includes *New Atlantis: A Narrative History of Scientific Romance* (Wildside Press, 2016), *The Plurality of Imaginary Worlds: The Evolution of French roman scientifique* (Black Coat Press, 2017) and *Tales of Enchantment and Disenchantment: A History of Faerie* (Black Coat Press, 2019). In support of the latter projects he has translated more than a hundred volumes of *roman scientifique* and more than twenty volumes of *contes de fées* into English.

His recent fiction, in the genre of metaphysical fantasy, includes a trilogy of novels set in West Wales, consisting of *Spirits of the Vasty Deep* (2018), *The Insubstantial Pageant* (2018) and *The Truths of Darkness* (2019), published by Snuggly Books.

CONTENTS

INTRODUCTION

AMOUR CHEMINE by Marie Krysinska (1857-1908), here translated as *The Path of Amour*,[1] was originally published in Paris by Alphonse Lemerre in 1892 and mostly consists of short stories initially published in *Gil Blas* and *La Lanterne* in 1889-91. It was the author's second publication in volume form, her first collection of poetry, *Rythmes pittoresques*, having been published by Lemerre in 1890 with an introduction by J. H. Rosny, gathering together materials published in various periodicals during the 1880s. The first of the addenda added to the story collection is taken from *Rythmes pittoresques*, where its date of composition is given as 1882, the second from *Le Capitan* in 1883, the third from *La Libre Revue* in 1884, and the fourth from *Le Figaro* in 1893. The remaining forty-four are taken from various issues of *La Fronde*, the pioneering feminist newspaper founded in 1897, edited and entirely written by women.

---

1 The verb *cheminer* signifies advancement, but is almost invariably used in French to signify advancement with difficulty. The original readers would have taken the implication that the path to be mapped out in the stories for the advancement of amour would be thorny.

Krysinska published two further volumes of "picturesque rhythms" and two novels in volume form, *Folle de son corps* (1896) and *La Force du Desir* (1905). An earlier novel, *Juliette Cordelin*, had only appeared as a feuilleton in *L'Éclair* in 1895. She continued to publish occasional short stories throughout the 1890s and into the early 1900s in such periodicals as *Gil Blas, La Lanterne* and *Journal pour tous*, but never assembled a second collection. The great majority of her prose contributions to newspapers after 1897 were in *La Fronde*, where she was given more editorial freedom to experiment thematically and stylistically, and for which she produced her most idiosyncratic work, routinely operating in a generic gray area where poetry in prose and short fiction overlap, and conducting interesting experiments in narrative minimalization.

The Warsaw-born author had initially come to Paris at the age of sixteen to study musical composition at the Conservatoire. She first began writing poetry to accompany her musical compositions, and published her work in numerous periodicals, including the one edited and published by habitués of the Chat Noir cabaret, where she became a regular. She was the only woman allowed to join Emile Goudeau's Hydropathes, and she subsequently joined the Zutistes, the "radical wing" of the cabaret's clientele. She often performed her work in the cabaret, either to her own piano accompaniment or that of Maurice Rollinat, alongside the likes of Jules Richepin and Edmond Haraucourt. She composed music to accompany the words of numerous other poets, including classic works by Charles Baudelaire and Victor Hugo as well as works by avantgardist contemporaries such as Charles Cros and Jean Lorrain. She also hosted a significant literary salon in her apartment in the Rue Monge. In 1885 she married the painter and lithographer Georges Bellenger (1847-1918) and she made two trips with him to the United States, the legacy of which is evident in three of the short stories in the present collection.

The idiosyncratic manner of her composition and performance led Krysinska to forsake standard rules of rhyme and scansion, and she became an important pioneer of *vers libre* [free verse], which involved her in a massive controversy when the Symbolist Gustave Kahn claimed to have invented *vers libre* and his cronies deliberately excluded Krysinska's name from the Symbolist Manifesto and their other writings—an insult that she took very hard, as she considered herself, quite rightly, to be a writer at the very heart of the Symbolist Movement. She spent a great deal of effort attempting to counter Kahn's alleged usurpation, with the aid of many of her literary friends. Although there was clear evidence of her priority, after Kahn had initially attempted to deny it, Édouard Dujardin contended that her supposed early works of *vers libre* were actually poems in prose—a plausible assertion, given that two of the key examples, "Les Fenêtres" (here translated as "Windows") and "Un Roman dane la lune" (tr. as "A Romance in the Moon"), were both given that label in the periodicals in which they appeared, although many of the other examples reprinted in *Rythmes pittoresques* are clearly and unambiguously examples of *vers libre*. The ambiguous works are, however, of considerable interest no matter what label is applied to them, in terms of the originality of their form, and Krysinska's subsequent stylistic experimentation involved the production of numerous other works crossing conventional boundaries. Her attempted exclusion and subsequent partial eclipse from "official" literary history is nowadays seen—accurately—as a monumental example of sexist injustice, and her important contribution to the history of French Symbolism is becoming more accurately recognized and celebrated.

By comparison with her musical compositions and her poetry, including her ventures into innovative prose poetry, many of Krysinska's short stories seem a trifle pedestrian, many of those in *Amour chemine* being ordinary examples of commercial work fitting the conventions established by prolific producers of short stories for newspapers such as Catulle Mendès and Octave Mirbeau. Some of those produced for *La Fronde* are also a trifle anodyne, but they were genuinely experimental in their terse and minimalistic narrative construction—or, in some instances, their deliberate lack of narrative construction—and the more elaborate examples have an effectively quirky wit.

The entire subgenre of *fin-de-siècle* newspaper short fiction tended to be cynically anti-romantic, routinely tending toward the laconic irony characteristic of the *conte cruel*, and Krysinska's work is no exception, but it is sometimes striking in its deft moral indifference, while occasionally providing a curious note of terminal uplift that counterbalances their generally jaundiced view of life, in a calculatedly perverse fashion. Interestingly, two of the stories from *Amour chemine* are very frank in representing the mythology of *fin-de-siècle* Bohemia as an illusion, suggesting that sleazy mundanity already had Paris firmly in its disabusing grip by 1891, at least outside the hallowed walls of the Chat Noir. It is in the stories and prose poems from *La Fronde*, however—by which time Parisian Bohemia was a thing of the past, already regarded with whimsical nostalgia—that her prose work acquired its greatest idiosyncrasy and distinction.

It is difficult to measure the extent of Krysinka's influence on the other regular contributors to *La Fronde*; given that they were fellow Symbolists and fellow feminists working with the same space restrictions, there was every reason to expect their work to have much in common. It seems probable, comparing the work of the authors who produced short fiction for the newspaper most prolifically in parallel with her, "May Armand Blanc" (the daughter of the sculptor Francis de Saint-Victor and the writer Mathilde de Saint-Victor) and "Jacques Fréhel" (Alice Télot), that they had as much influence on her as she had on them, but the three of them constituted a fascinating common endeavor. That endeavor did not last long—effectively covering some eighteen months from late 1898 to early 1900—but it nevertheless made considerable strides in pioneering a new area of literary activity carried out by women with a female audience in mind, to which Krysinska definitely made a substantial contribution as an exemplar and as an experimentalist.

Krysinska's prose only has occasional flashes of the determined flamboyance of the contemporary work of her friend Rachilde, the delicacy of Renée Vivien's prose poetry, or the exotic adventurism of Jane de La Vaudère's fiction, but its subtle feminism nevertheless provided a neat counterpoint to the frequent misogynistic contempt of many of the Chat Noir's regulars and their successors, and she took her mission in that regard seriously, backing it up with intelligence in her critical writings. She is certainly entitled to the place of honor in *fin-de-siècle* literary history that some of her contemporaries tried to deny her, and her prose work, although it was only the third string of her versatile bow, is worthy of sympathetic attention as well as being eminently readable. It certainly warrants preservation and modern critical interest.

This translation of *Amour chemine* was made from a PDF file obtained from the reproduction of the Lemerrre volume contained on Google Books. The translations in the appendix were all made directly from the versions of the texts reproduced on the Bibliothèque Nationale *gallica* website.

—Brian Stableford

THE PATH
OF
AMOUR

RATIONAL MARRIAGE

To M. Eugène Ledrain[1]

I

PHRASIE, the maid, comes to the lamps, and, at a sign from Madame she withdraws, after having foraged with the poker in the fireplace, where a rosy coke fire is burning under the fine lilac ashes.

Now Monsieur and Madame are alone in the familiar small drawing room where a delicate perfume of white heliotrope floats, the favorite perfume of Mademoiselle Lucie Bolène, who will soon have been passing for eight years as Jean Gautrin's wife but who is only his legitimate mistress, as she sometimes says, laughing, to her rare friends.

What need has she of friends?

Since Jean Gautrin offered her his arm at Royat to aid her mount up at Charade, she has always been slightly

---

1 Eugène Ledrain (1844-1910) was an Orientalist who made a new translation of the Bible, published by Alphonse Lemerre, and became the curator of Oriental artifacts at the Louvre

astonished when anyone informs her that there are other men in the world, other couples who also love one another, and yet others riveted together for life who are their reciprocal torment.

First there was the marvelous beginning of passion, of annihilating embraces and lethargic kisses, in which the young woman's nineteen years and the man's twenty-eight opened to the red sun of amour the powerful flower made of all the new and rich blood of their hearts.

But the years of tender calm that followed were sweeter still: the charming security of habit and communal life delightfully limited by the horizon of two faithful arms.

In the same small blue and gray drawing room with dormant mirrors and dreaming portraits, in which the open piano contains in its flanks the phantoms of beloved music, how many times, silently abandoned on the supple cushions of the divan, have they resuscitated the memories? Royat and its mountains, arching a back like good placid pets. And the excursions on perilous paths on intractable donkeys, which are headstrong, as is well-known—but what pretty heads, with large, malign dark eyes and ample susceptible ears, which one dare not touch in spite of their signal mildness.

God, how miraculously beautiful Lucie was, Jean Gautrin often thinks, *on the day when we hired Souris and Bichette to climb the Puy de Dôme. In spite of her futile little Parisienne's hat, she didn't want to open the umbrella, and she was right. Her crystalline eyes were mirrors of the joyful sky and her pale flowery complexion had no fear of the sun.*

Souris bent down continually to eat a thistle, doubtless convinced that it was uniquely for that reason that he had

4

been brought there. Then the amazon, in order to maintain her equilibrium, braced her hips with a lovely decisive movement, and gently inclined a noble nape of living gold, from which the blonde tresses sprang like a magnificent harvest.

But she is beautiful now, the fortunate lover does not fail to conclude; *her complexion has colored slightly and has become more similar to mine, and her beautiful sheaves of hair have darkened slightly, because mine is brown: the touching and mysterious effect of an intimate fusion of two beings.*

Lucie is thinking almost the same things, and she adds, mentally: *Isn't it curious that in Jean's admirable brown curls there are now golden reflections?*

This evening, Jean Gautrin is not thinking any of that. He even avoids looking at Lucie, and all the familiar details of that small blue and gray drawing room wound his eyes like swords.

The pink chine peignoir that Lucie is wearing produces the effect on his nerves of very sad music, such as the Chopin ballad in which the drama of some intimate treason unfurls in slow recitatives.

Will it be necessary to abandon the sweet Lucie, his wife—his true wife—in order to marry the haughty Geneviève Legrand, who does not spare him the marks of a glacial indifference, the image of his own sentiments for her? Is there no other means to bring about the fusion of two rival banks than that fatal marriage? And how is he going to announce it to Lucie? Into what tragic despair will it plunge the loving creature who gave herself to him so absolutely on the threshold of a young existence opening the most inviting perspectives before her?

With what bitterness he remembers the evening when Lucie, with her arms around his neck, told him that she had just cancelled a superb engagement in Russia and broken with a certain future of glory and fortune. With what passion for art she had sung that evening for him alone!

Oh, misery.

Only the thought that this marriage is an inevitable necessity gives him a semblance of courage to embark on an explanation as they go into the bedroom.

II

At the same moment, this is what is happening in the silent town house of the banker Legrand.

Geneviève, who was believed to be asleep in her young woman's bedroom, is awake and very melancholy. Tortured by insomnia she has quit the bed that gripped her with the relentless arms of an executioner and, without even thinking about covering her shoulders, thinned somewhat since this project of marriage, she lights the lamp again and sits on a corner of the divan, with the box containing her particular treasure on her knees.

There are, of course, dried flowers, portraits of school friends, her childhood rings, now too small for her fingers. But the portraits of friends only obtain a single glance this time, and nervous hands jostle them and send them into the corners of the box face down.

Genevieve has found what she was looking for: it is an excessively pink paper rose with silver foliage.

The effect of that insignificant find is a storm of tears shed by Mademoiselle Geneviève Legrand; for that rose is a memory of a dance, and it is Georges de Linières who gave it to her one winter evening when she thought she was living in a fairy tale.

The music, the flowers as brilliant as ball gowns and the costumes as fresh as flowers, all of that unreal and charming décor, is evoked with a crucifying complaisance, as well as the passionate words that Georges whispered in her ear, which made her heart palpitate for the first time beneath her corsage of tulle, like a little wild bird imprisoned by a child's hand.

She only knows now how much she loves him, since she knows that she must never see him again.

O infinite sadness!

And will it not be an impiety to promise before God, to the man who is to be her husband, that heart so completely given to another man? But to disobey her parents is also an impiety.

"Oh, my God, advise me!"

And Geneviève, by virtue of a habit acquired in childhood, falls to her knees next to her bed—above which a Christ opens his charitable arms, impotent against the ill will of human perversity—and tries to pray, while pressing against her emotional breasts the poor paper rose, which her tears have reduced to the state of a rag.

III

The marriage of Jean Gautrin with Mademoiselle Geneviève Legrand was celebrated at Sainte-Clotilde, on the radiant afternoon in May that is still remembered by all the free birds of Paris. Under a festival sky and amid the quivering foliage of lilacs, multitudes of couples flapped their wings, which is the formula customary among sparrows to swear amour and protection. And the great plane trees blessed them, swaying their branches majestically, but without emphasis.

In the sacristy, when all the ladies surrounded the bride in order to give her the obligatory embrace, Geneviève had the impression that friends and enemies were giving her the last kiss of pardon due to a dead woman.

Jean had a furious desire to challenge to a duel all the comrades who came to shake his hand and express their good wishes. Almost all of them had often come to sit down at the table of Mademoiselle Lucie Bolène, whom they called Madame Gautrin, and had made the inevitable comments about the excessively radiant happiness of the lovers.

Were they mocking him now with their good wishes?

In the carriage cluttered with white bouquets, when the husband and wife were seated, alone, they looked at one another with the particular acuity of perception of the decisive moments of life. The fortress of dolor in which

each of them was imprisoned became physically visible,
and a reciprocal pity became the first link, the unique
link, connecting those two beings condemned to love
one another.

IV

An entire year has fallen into the basket of Time, the
rag-picker who collects without discrimination the fresh
roses that were the blessed minutes, the pure gold of lost
happiness and the torn veils that envelop our mourning—
also forgotten, alas.

Monsieur and Madame Gautrin have the appearance
of any couple doing all that it is appropriate to do.

They even went to Royat together and—the mockery
of chance!—hired Souris and Bichette to make the ascen-
sion of the Puy de Dôme.

That happened two months after their marriage.

The duty of amour—for their reason is subject to the
old atavism of educations without simplicity—the duty
of amour was, for him, something like the obligation
to offer his arm to a lady to whom one has just been
introduced before passing into a dining room; for her
it was the obedience sworn to the husband. But in both
of them, in the best corner of the soul, the shade of an
amour denied wept, and proclaimed in a loud voice that
this was a sacrilege.

Having arrived at Royat in mid-season they could
only find one bedroom, and for the first time they slept
together.

Awakening in broad daylight gave rise to a bizarre sensation.

For Jean, Geneviève's brown hair on the pillow in the place where he had found Lucie's blonde tresses for eight years was like an error, and he wondered whether he ought not to flee, confused, making apologies to the stranger.

As for Geneviève, in her semi-slumber her cheeks lit up with a passionate dream, which was a revelation to her senses, previously dormant. *If Georges de Linières were my husband*, she said to herself, almost articulating the words, *I could have him close beside me, then, like this?*

The high mountain that they could see through the window hid the sky. With its green dress trailing in a gentle slope, it was sitting so close to them that it seemed to be holding them on its knees.

And Jean recalled an identical impression next to Lucie one morning. But now, the mountain had the effect on him of a procuress.

Today, all that is already a memory.

The result of that year has, what is more, been rather unexpected.

Jean has felt as if every day were wrapping him increasingly in indifference. He has scarcely been moved by the recent catastrophe in which a million of their fortune was lost. A few hours later he surprised himself saying aloud: "What can all that matter to me?"

He has a clearer memory of the evening when he ran like a lunatic to the apartment of Lucie Bolène, whom he had not seen again since his marriage. He ran there, no longer having the strength to struggle against that amour. On the way, in the fiacre, he sobbed.

He remembers the alarmed expression of Phrasie, coming to open the door.

"Lucie is dead," he said, with the sang-froid of a man who has finally concluded his life.

But Lucie was not dead. It was much worse.

"Oh, it's good, I certify to you that it's very good," he said, laughing very singularly, as he went into his club an hour later.

"Tell us, since it's so good."

"I've just been to see one of my good friends . . . one of my best friends, I ought to say . . ." And that singular laugh punctuated the words in a rather ludicrous manner, for in sum, the fact of seeing even one's best friend has nothing so amusing about it.

So they only found a mediocre "goodness" in it, and returned all their momentarily-distracted attention to the baccarat. However, Jean Gautrin continued: "And where did I find him, that excellent friend? In whose home?"

But no one was listening, and Jean Gautrin, like the others, soon started gambling with the others, for high stakes.

Furthermore, he was astonishingly lucky. But while he was laying down the nines and the eights he had in his ears the little fearful cry that Lucie had uttered on seeing him, and seeing again her pink peignoir, which would have taken flight without that excellent friend who forced her to receive Jean Gautrin. After a slight disturbance—very comprehensible, was it not?—Lucie Bolène recovered her calm and the two lovers welcomed Jean Gautrin very politely and very cheerfully, as befitted happy people.

He called her "darling" and she called him "dear."

Then Jean no longer thought about anything, only following the fall of the cards with an extraordinary attention. He could not remember ever having lent such attention to anything else in the world.

And Geneviève?

Geneviève no longer remembered anything,

Her life commenced on that day of last October. It was three months ago.

Was it really three months . . . ? Or three hours . . . ? Or three lifetimes.

She has seen Georges de Linières again as dusk was falling like golden snow.

How that soft and unique dusk fell and whirled with the dead leaves in that path in the Luxembourg, which certainly had nothing real about it.

At first she remained alone there for a long time, alone with a sky draped in plaintive tones. Then she was alone there with him, and with the sky that had suddenly become sumptuous and clad in joy.

Oh, it was not memories that were evoked.

Memories? They had none.

It was a candid and glorious nativity of amour.

And they understood that it would be impious not to belong to one another.

V

After a night spent at the club, Jean Gautrin returned home as day was beginning to break. He reflected in the pitiful result produced, in sum, by that marriage of two social reasons—an action from which, at least from the practical point of view, one had the right to expect marvels.

Nothing was better imagined than that association. And, in fact, in the first week, several small bankers failed, devoured by the colossus Gautrin and Legrand. But what changes in a year!

Jean Gautrin, melancholy and distracted, had made blunder after blunder, and the capital, at the present moment, was massively depleted.

Then he gambled recklessly, only finding real distraction at the club, and luck had not been as constant as Lucie.

Before the threat of ruin, he thought about Geneviève with a tenderness in which rancor against Lucie played no small part.

As he approached the house his attention was attracted by a fiacre stationed a few feet from his door.

Then that very door opened and a feminine shadow glided at a somnambulistic pace toward the fiacre, into which it disappeared.

The fiacre drew away immediately, and was swallowed up by the bleak space of the deserted early morning streets, in which only the sound of the street sweepers whipped the silence.

Jean remained motionless, in spite of the bitter cold of the dawn. A strange hallucination caused his mind to vacillate. Had not that shadow had the gait and stature of his wife?

But he laughed aloud at that absurdity, went swiftly up to his room and went to bed.

His overtaxed nerves caused him to turn in the icy sheets like a piece of wreckage tossed by the waves.

The window, inundated by the daylight, rising surprisingly blue and cruel, gave the impression of a broad steel blade sharpened for executions.

And he was oppressed by the special sadness inflicted on human beings every time they transgress the holy laws of the Norm and try to flee the glorious morning light into the lairs of a bad Slumber after having dilapidated the calming treasure of the Night.

Nevertheless, he ended up going to sleep.

Meanwhile, the express carried Geneviève and George de Linières away, enlaced in an irrevocable embrace.

INGENUOUSNESS

American Mores

To M. Henry Bauër.[1]

MRS. ROBERTSON lingered voluptuously in the bathroom, next to the bath, where the opaline water, perfumed with Florida Water, was still oscillating slightly. In the narrow mirror hanging on the wall in front of her she saw, lost in curlers, her pretty white and pink face, which she confessed pleasurably, was as pretty as the pictures smiling on Mr. Reynolds' cigarette boxes. She pronounced that name in a whisper, adding the forename David, and repeated several times: "David Reynolds." It sounded like exquisite music, and evoked the face of her lover, joyful and correct, with a fine blond

---

1 "Henry Bauër" was the signature used by the journalist Henri Bauër (1851-1915), a natural son of Alexandre Dumas and a Communard exiled to New Caledonia before becoming the theater critic of the *Écho dc Paris*. Like several of the other dedicatees in the present collection, he supported Krysinska's claim to be the true pioneer of *vers libre* in her famous dispute with Gustave Kahn and his fellow Symbolists.

15

moustache. Mrs. Robertson rolled over in memories of intoxication like a cat on a carpet.

At that moment, someone knocked on the door. She replied: "All right," while finishing lacing her corset methodically.

It was Mr. Robertson, her husband, who was reminding her that the time was approaching to meet their friends for the excursion to City Point.

✳

At five past two, at the corner of Common Garden, the Robertson household met the company composed by Mr. Reynolds and Mr. and Mrs. Armstrong, with their fourteen-year-old daughter, whom they were taking to a party for the first time.

The two gentlemen took out their watches at the same time and made the observation to the Robertsons that they were five minutes late—which is a serious matter in the United States.

After waiting for a few minutes, during which the conversation was limited to a unanimous observation of the fine weather, the sound of bells announced the desired tram. Soon they were comfortably seated in the ingenious and comfortable vehicle answering to the name of a "car," entirely trellised, with benches disposed sideways, as in a concert hall. The driver, dressed like an embassy attaché, standing up, governed with gravity two rapid and strong horses, which bore the light, elegant and long vehicle without difficulty.

Mr. Reynolds was placed between Mrs. Robertson and little Lizzie, who, in her joy at finally being on the way to City Point, almost leapt on to the gentleman's knees, sitting down too abruptly; then, without being disturbed in the slightest, she passed on to another kind of exercise. Bursting into laughter, she showed her mother the fantastic hat and outrageous make-up of a fake beauty who had just sat down at the other end of the tram, in the part reserved for smokers, where Mr. Robertson and Mr. Armstrong were installed, cigars in their teeth.

Mrs. Robertson, whose arm was quivering at being lightly pressed against that of Mr. Reynolds, followed with moist and distracted eyes the familiar details of Tremont Street, which is the principal street of Boston.

The red houses with green shutters, further brightened by the white sheets that the housewives hung on ropes above the roof terraces, which the air was inflating, causing them to float like the sails of ships.

In places, in the midst of skirts, into which the wind put the comical ballooning of imaginary bellies, a pair of black stockings danced a jig.

Then came the shop signs.

An enormous pipe in the colors of the United States announces—by virtue of some unknown symbolism—a hairdresser's shop. In front of tobacconists' shops, Indian women in painted wood—the last vestige of the former American people—present passers-by with packets of fat cigars or blocks of chewing-tobacco, with a half-smile on their varnished faces, from which the nose is often missing, while the excessive calves, the mauve nudity of which is ornamented by gilded rings, are poised for illusory departures.

Telegraph poles, in thousands, file past in the inverse direction to the tram, like the skeletons of long fish hastening about their business.

Lizzie must have been bitten by a mosquito—those beasts are terrible in Boston—for she was agitating in an unusual fashion in her little white flannel tennis blouse.

Mr. Reynolds, occupied in learning by heart a corner of the nape of Mrs. Robertson's neck, was extracted from that state by the movements of the little girl, who had just elbowed him in the stomach.

He looked at Lizzie for the first time and perceived that she was very pretty.

How had the unpleasant eyes of Mr. Armstrong, the color of rusty old coins, been able to become, in his daughter, that pair of superb brown eyes with cheerful lashes, and how had the salted herring mouth of Mrs. Armstrong, with its downturned corners, been transfigured in her daughter into that lush moist fruit, in which the little milky almond teeth were as tempting as candy?

That was what Mr. Reynolds was saying to himself while Mrs. Robertson pressed his knee with hers nervously, but without her face losing anything of its joyous placidity. She was even telling Mrs. Armstrong, animatedly, about her troubles as a housewife.

The tram was now rolling through the poor and populous neighborhoods. A multitude of barefoot children with unkempt hair were swarming in the dirty streets, accumulating in groups like flies in order to enjoy themselves noisily, crouching in the midst of banana skins and peelings of all kinds strewn on the ground. The majority, negro or half-caste, as merry as young monkeys, were making comically awkward gestures, while the children of Irish immigrants retained an unconscious elegance under their rags and charming British baby-clothes.

They were approaching the sea, and fishmongers were abundant. Octopodes cut into pieces filled baskets with their creamy flesh; living lobsters, fully armed, dragged themselves stupidly over beds of seaweed, dappled with pieces of ice, seeing to hold funereal discussions with their cooked brethren, clad in sinister crimson.

An iodine odor floated in the air, overheated by the incendiary sunlight of the American summer. The intoxicating perfume of pineapples and bananas mingled with it as they passed the displays of fruits set up in the open air by Italians.

Finally, they arrived at the beach of City Point, which is not a rendezvous of fashionable bathers, like Nantucket, but an unpretentious beach, little frequented during the week, and not at all organized for bathing—only the children of the neighboring districts and little barelegged girls splash around in shallow places, and then return to the shore and dry themselves like young dogs, by running. Their silhouettes, which stand out vigorously against the luminous sea, make one think of those unmodeled Etruscan paintings, so impressive by virtue of the physiognomy of gesture.

Young boys were digging in the moist sand with their knives in order to extract clams, which they ate raw. The women also wanted to have those shellfish, and the gentlemen, rolling up their sleeves, started digging in the mud while smoking their cigars.

Suddenly, Miss Lizzie, forgetting what she owed to her spick and span costume, ran to crouch down next to Mr. Reynolds and also began digging with her little schoolgirl's pen-knife, her hands and arms in the mud.

At each clam she cried out: "Look! Look!" showing it to Mr. Reynolds, her cheeks pink with pleasure, while that gentleman's gaze went automatically to the fine black stockings that her mischievous pose uncovered all the way to the knees, where the snowy embroidery of her bloomers began.

Mrs. Robertson, rather irritated by that game, launching angry glances at her lover, ended up saying: "That's enough clams! Shall we go for a walk?"

But Lizzie was having too much fun, and did not want to hear it. Mr. Reynolds was not bored either.

Lizzie made the decision to send her straw hat to get bogged down further away, like a little stranded boat, and her curls, gilded by the sun, resembled flames caressing her milky skin, like Chinese porcelain, which her narrow forehead and pretty little Saxon nose, pert and pure, satined delicately.

Mr. Reynolds found her exquisite, and the child perceived that quite clearly. Besides which, Mr. Reynolds pleased her greatly, perhaps because he admired her, and perhaps also because he resembled a painting she had seen in a large art-dealer's shop.

Her frolics came to an end, however, and she was taken to the edge of the sea to wash her hands.

Lizzie's handkerchief was soaked before her arms were duly wiped, and Mr. Reynolds lent her his, richly perfumed, which Miss Lizzie kept for far longer than necessary. That perfume, in which musk and tobacco were mingled, dazzled and intoxicated her delightfully. When she returned it to the gentleman, who never ceased to savor her with his eyes, she discovered that she was quite simply madly in love with Mr. Reynolds.

Mrs. Robertson found a means to leave her husband behind with the Armstrong household and took Mr. Reynolds' arm.

She was pale with chagrin, but her eyes retained their habitual soft gaze.

She had, in any case, never been more infatuated with her lover. Her lips were thirsty for kisses, and jealousy exasperated her desires, which went toward that man with a humiliated and fervent ardor.

"Dear, darling," she murmured, without being able to find anything but those tender words, instead of everything haughty that she had prepared in order to punish him when she was able to speak to him.

Mr. Reynolds, for his part, recovered from his strange disturbance of a little while before and pressed the arm of his mistress passionately, finding her more charming with that reckless and docile gaze.

She had recaptured him entirely, and they walked silently, overwhelmed by a tender languor.

The translucent blue firmament was traversed by long golden streaks, of which no vapor diminished the purity, and the sea, shimmering like the plumage of turtle-doves, seemed to be asleep between the amorous arms of the horizon, where islets with green hills dressed the intense sapphire.

The diaphanous sails of fishing boats floated like extended wings, steeped in rosy hues at the edge of the sky.

"Tell me that you're sorry for having caused me chagrin," said Mrs. Robertson, in a voice in which all the bitter melancholy whined of not being able to belong forever, without division, to the man she loved, while the footsteps of her husband, behind her, desolated her ears.

"But in what way have I caused you chagrin, dear heart?" replied Mr. Reynolds, playing the good apostle with a hypocrisy that almost went as far as sincerity, so much did he persuade himself of his admirable innocence.

"Now, now, don't flirt with my wife," said Mr. Robertson, approaching. "She's a terrible flirt, don't you know?"

"I know, I know," replied Mr. Reynolds, smiling placidly and releasing Mrs. Robertson's arm in order to surrender it to her husband.

It was a matter of deciding where they would have dinner, and that question absorbed the whole company for a few moments.

They ended up choosing one of the restaurants near the jetty, and they headed in that direction. But this time, it was Lizzie who gave her arm to Mr. Reynolds, and their confounded silhouettes were visible—some way ahead—outlined against the sky, which was becoming fulgurant.

✳

A week later, Mrs. Robertson finished setting her curls free, the curlers of which fluttered like beautiful gilded moths, in order to assemble them on top of her head: an American coiffure that has something of the clown and something of the archangel about it.

Mrs. Robertson was getting ready to visit Mr. Reynolds, whom she had not seen since the excursion to City Point, when someone knocked on the door.

"Come in!" the young woman responded, with a shudder, and her friend Mrs. Armstrong soon offered herself to her gaze, which was nothing less than distressed by that spectacle, above all at that moment.

Out of breath, Mrs. Armstrong unfolded a letter, which she almost tore to pieces in her emotion. Finally, she held it out to Mrs. Robertson without making any comment, and this is what Mrs. Robertson deciphered:

> *Dear Mama, this is to tell you that I have*
> *had enough of school and being a little girl.*
> *I love David Reynolds and he is already my*
> *husband. We are going to Chicago for a week.*
> *As soon as we return we will come to embrace*
> *you and papa, as always.*
> *Lizzie Reynolds.*

Mrs. Armstrong, very agitated, but fundamentally glad, paced back and forth on the bedroom carpet saying:

"Oh, Lord! These things happen every day, I know, but I'm alarmed all the same. Such a young girl. The little Davidson girl—do you know her?—last year, was only sixteen, and Lizzie isn't yet fifteen. Anyway, David Reynolds has a good position!" she concluded, letting herself fall into a rocking chair, whose seesaw agitated frenetically. "But you've known Mr. Reynolds for a long time," she went on, without noticing Mrs. Robertson's pallor and disturbance. "He's a friend, isn't he?"

At that point she softened, and, getting to her feet with the abruptness of a spring, while the rocking chair, relieved of her weight, swung furiously, she took her interlocutor's hands and cooed in her face, with an apocryphal emotion: "He's a worthy dear man, isn't he, and my Lizzie will be happy?"

"Yes, she certainly will be . . . happy, certainly," replied Mrs. Robertson, prey to unspeakable tortures and making a superhuman effort to retain her mild and placid gaze.

THE RIVAL

To M. Georges Montorgueil.[1]

ABOARD the American steamer *Pennland*, two hours out of Antwerp, the travelers, all on deck were following with their eyes and binoculars what could still be seen of the continent, a great scaffolding of hills flattening out and disappearing like a stage set removed by the scene-shifters.

Marc Deslandes, his back to the bulwark, examined the people with whom he would be closely mingled for all hours for more than a week during the crossing. The majority were American families returning for the winter to the fold of Broadway and the august bosom of business, after having contemplated, on the faith of tourist guides, the most remarkable things in the Old World.

Men in ludicrous traveling costumes and hideous double-peaked caps seemed to have escaped from a bad

---

1 "Georges Montorgueil" was the best-known pseudonym of the journalist Octave Lebesgue (1857-1933), who worked, like several of the other dedicatees, for the *Écho de Paris* in the late 1880s and early 1890s.

vaudeville, and Marc wondered whether life was not striving to imitate the false interpretations that the theater made of it. The wind from the sea made the veils of women flutter; they had an anonymous character that prevented Marc from imagining them alive outside the boat, living an intimate life; he was tempted to believe that they only existed while traveling.

Marc Deslandes had quit the "capital of pleasures" a few days before to escape a commencement of spleen that he had decided not to allow to settle in under any pretext, having a great fear of being "new school." He went to explore the museums of Holland, full of masterpieces glorifying, with robust and tender tones, good health, good faith and good humor, all things disreputable and considered "old hat" at the present time.

Those masters, admirable in naïve and savant passion, and patient effort, from Van Eyck to Jordaens, provided such a marvelous cure that Marc woke up one morning with the desire for a sea voyage, in order to respire the powerful saline wind beneath the broad sky.

It was an opportunity to go to visit a married sister in New York, who would have a pleasant surprise, believing him to be engrossed in amusements and stories of women.

Women! Oh, that was the black spot! He had found, like others, mistresses who loved him "very much" and proved it by oppressing him with the little annoyances of a graceful animal, not understanding anything about anything, or sentimental stupidities that made his hair stand on end—but he did not conclude from that, with Schopenhauer, the total deception of amour, knowing that a truly remarkable woman and a man of genius are two blackbird of equal whiteness.

Marc had obtained from his mother a little Oriental blood, which rendered utterly insupportable to him the precarious pittance picked up in his amorous adventures and caused him to emerge from every intrigue disappointed, dreaming of a creature as beautiful and as silent as the Night, who would overwhelm him with unforgettable sensualities. It seemed to him that only one, but absolute, abandonment of himself between the arms of such a being, a plenitude of conquered intoxication, might put to sleep that nostalgia for divine fulgurance, which enraged him with sadness in the midst of pitiful simulations. He also believed that if it were given to him to encounter one day the being summoned for such a long time by all the voices of his soul and flesh, dying of thirst for amour, he would infallibly recognize her—which was equivalent to saying that he believed in the famous "thunderbolt." Marc Deslandes was decidedly "old hat."

The ocean lost its glaucous tone of coastal waters, taking on the solid color and heavy aspect of lead, evoking epic and glorious plains after fabulous combats, in which the shields of dead heroes were resplendent in the sunlight

Marc thought now about visiting his cabin. He went down the carpeted stairway, lost himself in the narrow corridors of a drunken and unsteady house in which the purr of the engines aggravated vertigo and disconcerted

the nerves. Suddenly, on turning a corner, a pitch of the vessel positively threw a young woman into his arms.

The effect was formidable, for he immediately saw that it was *her*.

And while she remained pressed against him, without astonishment, he recognized the voluptuous eyes as somber as evening, the gilded and smooth skin, like a page of a missal illuminated by the blood of lips.

Now, a little confusion came to them—the sensation of an awakening.

Marc offered his arm, which was simply accepted, and they went back up on deck, where the passengers, packaged in plaids and blankets, were already collapsing into the deckchairs.

Sitting at the rear of the boat, Marc and his encounter chat like friends.

Eve Signeulle—that is the stranger's name—is a cantatrice and she is going to New York, where she has an engagement at the Opera House. She has decided on that partly to see new lands but mostly to flee a former and detested lover who does not want to resign himself,

Marc pales at the idea that another has dared to possess that body, which is given to him in every glace.

"Oh, how I have waited for you," he says.

"Me too," she replies.

At that moment the sea is like a blue pasturage with errant white goats on the horizon; closer, the largest waves, like free horses, are shaking their manes of foam and bounding with loud whinnies. A flock of seagulls fills the sky with loud cries, sometimes descending so close over the vessel that their heads can be seen turning, in a little child-like and determined movement, their wings outspread, almost motionless.

✳

Marc and the young woman did not quit one another for a single moment. They had become their reciprocal reason for living. When they separated for the night it seemed to them to be an injustice of God. Was it not evident that they were married, both in their souls melting with tenderness and their flesh sobbing with desires?

Marc spent an atrocious night. It appeared derisory to him to return to his cabin, where two horrible men were already asleep. One, his scarf knotted around his head, resembled a bearded old woman, the other was suffering from a resounding catarrh complicated by sea-sickness.

His beloved Eve was sleeping a few paces away, in the company of ridiculous women.

Was it not monstrous to be unable to possess her to the rocking of the great Torment roaring with amour, in spite of the fecundation of Eternities?

The next day, when they found one another again, the touch of her hand calmed him, and her little teeth, when she spoke, seeming drops of milk drawn from the gazelles of Paradise, refreshed the fever of his eyes.

One day, above the rail of the spar-deck, they plunged a pitying gaze at the group of emigrants collapsed on the deck with the fixed, almost hieratic, attitudes that long discouragements leave. The Italians most of all, with red shawls and yellow shirts in bright cotton, and the faded yellow jackets of pifferari, evoked a heart-rending and ruined Naples, with the regret of its joyful sky . . .

Then there were a few Germans, porcelain pipes screwed into their teeth, with outmoded hats.

On the gray and brown sea, like infinite extents of sterile heathland convulsed by cataclysms, the ship swayed the sonorous framework of its flanks, sliding into the massive watery valleys and climbing above the horizon again, which then seemed to be falling into gulfs. Giant walls of iron surged forth but sank immediately, with a mighty voice, into the natal Chaos. In the firmament, long black clouds were borne like stretchers on the shoulders of the trade winds.

The sailors hauled in the sails uttering rhythmic and barbaric ululations like the very plaint of the elements, in eternal sorrow beneath the implacable skies.

A cabin boy was washing the white-painted iron bars of the bulwark, a Flemish cabin boy with the face of an angel—but an angel who had rolled around all the taverns of the ports. When he saw Eve leaning on Marc's arm, watching with compassion a poor woman leaning against the rigging like a parcel of despair and sobbing into her brown hands he approached the couple to explain it.

"You know, the Italian woman you can see who is weeping—well, her child died yesterday morning and the shark has been following the ship all day, waiting for the body to be buried at sea—to eat it, you know; and when there's someone dead on the ship the shark knows it, and follows the ship; it's always like that, you know."

Eve and Marc felt fingernails cold with horror on their skin.

Death! They had not yet thought of that. Death between them one day . . . was that possible? Was that just?

Oh, but how they would have sacked and pillaged all the treasures of delight beforehand; ecstasies such that, on awakening from embraces, they would be astonished still to be alive after so much joy.

Three days more and they would reach land. No matter what land—it was the Canaan promised to their long desire. Marc was almost maddened by it. Oh, would it not have been easy for him to take her, his Eve, even if she had belonged to an extra-legitimate husband and three hundred and sixty-five families jealous of their rights? He had won her sufficiently by virtue of infinite tortures endured for a week. But Eve was free, and she loved him.

That evening they took their customary place at the poop of the ship and remained there for a long time. The sea was phosphorescent, and in the wake labored by the propeller, fruits and flowers of fire opened, burst, died and were reborn. And they thought they were seeing the trailing robe, fringed with humid stars, of the conquering Night.

The firmament was constellated with the bivouac fires of nomadic Infinity.

And the rigging of the vessel, furled sails, flew in the sky, seeming to climb it, leaving the splashing sea, already far beneath, to rage furiously.

Marc held his beloved tightly enlaced. The anguish of his senses became such that he threw himself upon her mouth and her neck, bruising her with furious kisses that rendered her gasping with amour, half-fainted in his arms.

Returned to themselves, they inspected the surroundings anxiously, but all the passengers had gone back in; those who were not in bed were playing whist in the lounge.

Only the sailors on watch were parading their heavy silhouettes, dragging in their wake the strong odor of tar.

They enlaced again, drowning one another with kisses, rolling as if in a lake of sensuality, in the suffering of desiring one another in vain.

Suddenly, Eve uttered a cry, putting her hand to her breast.

"What's wrong, my beloved?" asked Marc.

"Nothing . . . it's nothing . . . merely too much happiness."

✳

The next day, at dawn, Marc went to walk on deck. The night had been infernal but the cool air cured him.

In the pure sky, there were avalanches of roses and linen soaked in fresh blood: what remained of a singular and gallant drama.

More roses rolled in the waves in the midst of gems, diffuse at first and then—the sun had risen—bursting like a fanfare of sparks like a folly of light.

At that moment the ship's doctor approached him with the attitude of a pauper asking for a sou, and said to him, stammering: "It's necessary for you to have courage Monsieur Deslandes. Mademoiselle Signeulle died this morning of a ruptured aneurism."

Then, seeing the other utterly immobile, he went on: "Such a young woman . . . it's desolating; she must have had a very strong emotion. I advise you to shut yourself in your cabin in order not to witness the lugubrious spectacle of the burial at sea."

As Marc did not respond with a single word, the doctor drew away.

His two hands riveted to the rail, without a thought, Marc felt the toothed wheel of dementia rotating in his head.

But the vision of *Her*, surprisingly clear, imposed itself and saved him, throwing him to his knees in a torrent of tears.

His front against the bar, he wept endlessly.

He was now a dolor prostrate before *her* memory with a tremulous respect and a tenderness, as if for a virgin who was his dear sister, known always.

A noise in the water made him raise his head with a gesture of exhaustion.

A cavalier was riding the waves, putting the foam to flight. Brilliant and sleek, in a black satin costume with a white waistcoat of the most gallant effect, he was bounding marvelously over the hollow wave in which his vigorous and charming body was reflected.

With a joyful grace he was following the ship, so closely that one could have caressed him, but for the rapidity of his dives.

The caresser! Oh, certainly, desire might come to more than one beauty. More than one, doubtless, would have loved to be eaten by kisses by that handsome follower.

And he was—I swear to you—a redoubtable rival.

He was the Shark.

RANCOR

To M. Aurélien Scholl.[1]

THE young and pretty Madame Robert Thalès had been attracting the admiration of bourgeois salons for a year while wearing her mourning, almost giving the husbands of her friends the desire to die—for how sweet it would be to know that one was regretted thus!

Oh yes, it was with authentic tears that she wept for her dear Robert, the poor Left-Alone! And the memories of two years of conjugal paradise lacerated her heart, inspiring in her, in spite of her piety something like hatred for the Executioner God who, after having taken the beloved, left her all the cruel memories of intoxication . . .

The fact is that the Lord could not have had a more unfortunate hand on the day of distributions of Crosses when he sent a harsh widowhood to that amorous bird, who had an atrocious little character—and of resignation, not a shadow.

---

1 The writer and journalist Aurélien Scholl (1833-1902), long-time editor of the *Écho de Paris*.

Raised by parents pagan in ecstasy before their unique child; habituated even to the adoration of her companions in study, who were subject to the joyful charm of her spiritual, eccentric and sumptuous beauty, with her heavy tresses positively woven in gold, Louise, now the widowed Madame Thalès, could not conceive that anyone could oppose her—much less cause her a great pain.

Now, it was her Robert, her beloved Robert, who had dared to cause her that frightful chagrin by leaving, when she wanted him there, beside her. Could she believe it, even today, before that deserted bed, which had witnessed so much joy?

And how he was able to imagine lovely awakenings, in favorite flowers that were found warm next to the breasts on which they were gently placed, at the same time as a bouquet of silent kisses!

How could he bear to leave her weeping now—so bitterly—calling to him in vain in a lamenting voice during the tragic nights of the end of October?

What was the point, then, of having said to her that she was his dear little wife, and his queen of infallible wishes?

What good was it to know that her slightest caprices had been adored, since he permitted her to be desolate today? And how cold she was, far from his faithful arms!

And an anger came to her for the poor shade, too beloved. Her dolor, by virtue of the force of intensity, almost became hatred.

✳

For example, there was young Charles de Presle, who was very well received when his love for the widow extracted a lament from him.

He knew, certainly, that his amour was hopeless. But to forbid himself to love that Louise, of whom he had been dreaming since he had attained the age of reason—which is to say, the age of dreams—he could not do it.

And then, his intimate chagrin had become a cherished habitude.

When he found Louise married—on his return from Tonkin, where he had covered himself in glory for her—he regretted not having left his life in the Annamite silos.

Then he departed again, far away, not doubting that absence, now that the sweet lighthouse of Promises no longer shone, would kill him or kill his amour.

Absence had not killed either one; and now he had found his beloved in tears, afflicted as much as him, and devoid of hope, like him.

How sweet that was! For Louise welcomed her childhood friend with all the innocent joy of which her dolorous heart was capable.

Sometimes, however—oh, rarely!—the Viper Hope brushed the heart of the poor amorous fellow.

How was it believable, in fact, that that beautiful vivacious plant, the charming Louise, would never flower again for amour?

When the widow divined that conflict of sentiments, all her amity for Charles de Presle fell into an infinite scorn, and she would have sent him away if she had had an atom of pity.

That morning in November, Louise went to his "home"—
to the cemetery.

She took him sheaves of sweet violets, damp with the
perfumed tears of the night and also the tears dearest to
the deceased: the faithful tears wept by the friend.

A truly admirable Peace slept beneath the leafless
branches, and the footsteps of pious visitors treading the
dry leaves did not trouble that melancholy ecstasy.

Louis felt less sad while very close to him, in that landscape mute with respect before their tenderness, stronger
than Death.

The chrysanthemums blooming in that funereal
garden were, without a doubt, the silent and symbolic
speech of the Beloved, retained under the earth, far from
her, by the narrow tyranny of God.

Did the white chrysanthemums not say that that
powerful Amour, now become saintly through Dolor,
was the pure Fountain springing all the way to the vaults
of Heaven?

Were those mauve corollas not plaintive words, words
of regret for their cherished intimate life, so brief?

And the pink chrysanthemums, as if tinted by the
blood of the heart that had only beaten for her, oh,
without a doubt they were the nostalgic remembrance of
intoxications, and the haunting of kisses.

At that moment, all her appeasement collapsed, and
an acute dolor, an insupportable, almost physical dolor,
oppressed all the fibers of the frail little being, wrath-

ful and willful, crucified by the despotic desire for that beloved flesh, identified with her flesh, and which would NEVER AGAIN be hers!

The tender affliction had been exasperated to the extent of revolt, to the extent of rancor, and she fled, sobbing.

Oh, the cruel man! How he is allowing me to suffer!

On returning home, half demented, she found Charles de Presle. He had come to bring her a few books; but, thinking that it would be impious even to talk about amity to that person Wounded by Amour, he was about to leave after having kissed her black-gloved fingers, when Louise, bewildered, streaming with tears, threw herself into his arms, saying: "I want to be yours . . . to avenge myself on *that wretch* . . . who is making me too unhappy!"

THE BLUE BIRD

To Monsieur Félicien Champsaur.[1]

MY very dear Germaine,
I have finally found the blue bird about which we talked so much in the convent: Happiness.[2]

I have found it in a fulgurant amour, as splendid as a sun.

Yes, your friend, who has been assassinating you for three years with pessimistic letters, *has a lover.*

Don't utter loud cries, dear, very dear Germaine. You have also found your blue bird, and, quite simply, you have received him from your mother's hands: a husband who adores you and whom you love passionately. But I

---

1 The novelist and journalist Félicien Champsaur (1858-1934) was another supporter of Krysinska in her crusade to be recognized as the pioneer of *vers libre*, who endorsed her claim in print.

2 This story predates by more than a decade Maurice Maeterlinck's famous play *Le Oiseau bleu* (1908), featuring a quest for the blue bird of happiness, which became the basis of a notable opera and a movie. The symbolic title had, however, been used in more than one musical play in the first half of the century, most notably an 1836 *féerie* credited to Jean Bayard and Antoine Varnier.

no longer have a mother and you know the melancholy life that I have led since I have been searching for the famous blue bird.

Oh, Lord, it isn't suitors that were lacking; but the monstrous fortune with which I was burdened at birth put me in mortal suspicion of any tender word and made me flee, fearfully, before a declaration. And then, when I thought I perceived a sincere passion—after all, I'm young, and no uglier than anyone else—that wasn't sufficient; I wanted to love myself, and it isn't as easy as vain people think to find someone one can love.

The man I love doesn't even know my name. So the homage of his love has given me a superhuman intoxication. It even seems to me that he thinks that I'm something of a slut, and I put a heroic determination into keeping him unaware of the fact that it was a virgin that he held in his arms last night.

I don't know his name either. But I know that I belong to him until death. And if my beloved cannot be my husband, well, he'll be my lover and I shall never marry.

There is no law human or divine, that can give me without sacrilege to someone I don't love or make me renounce someone I love.

So, don't be terrified for me, my very dear Germaine, you who have been more than a sister to me and who have been able to soften the sorrow of being alone in the world since childhood.

The amour that possesses me is so strong that it is holy, and God will not even have to pardon me for it.

Quickly, give me news of your own happiness. Your husband was obliged to travel. Has he returned?

How I would like to know him, and how I regret not having put more urgency into visiting you in our retreat in the year that you have been married. But it is necessary for me to confess it? Your happiness appeared to me so perfect that I was almost afraid of being jealous.

Now we each have our blue bird.

Only yours is as blue as the pure azure of a summer sky, while mine is blue like flames.

I embrace you with all my heart my dear, my very dear, Germaine.

Your faithful friend
Berthe Lestrange.

P.S. Reply to me quickly at the Terminus Hotel in Marseille.

✳

Having finished the letter, Berthe was about to put it in an envelope when her vanquisher approached her and, putting his arm round her supple and high waist—free under the elegant peignoir in an old rose crêpe de chine—and drew her seductively toward the inviting divan, where their embrace languished, ecstatically, careless of everything that was beyond the marvelous horizon of their amour.

It was truly one of those despotic passions, revealed to both of them with a brutal lightning suddenness, and against which it would have been as absurd and vain to try to struggle as it would have been to struggle against the elements.

After a lunch taken in their room, in which the bread, the wine and everything else had a paradisal taste because of the profound contentment of their senses, they went to delight in the sun on the jolly Canebière, which seems—after our pensive and gray northern cities—a reservoir of powerful and placid life: true life, with the charming cynicism of its joy and the strength of its repose.

When they were sitting under a veranda in front of two cups of coffee, of which their nerves had a terrible need, more than one passer-by turned round naively in order to admire the perfect grace of the couple.

Both tall, they had in their forms the equilibrium that characterizes individuals of an ancient and pure race.

In Berthe the signs of an irrefutable atavism were visible most of all in the almost hieratical beauty of the face, its tranquil lines, its eyes as blue as a precious stones, whose gaze penetrated further than discreet vision.

In him, the origin was translated less definably, in the mannerisms and as if by an ambience of noble stamp; for the superb brown eyes had an anxious melancholy and the vaguely ironic mouth lacked serenity.

It was also evident that both of them were miraculously endowed for amour.

Berthe revealed that gift, to the point of being disturbing for anyone who saw it, buy the undulating and supple design of her upper body, with slightly flexed shoulders, as if burdened, and by the color of her palely gilded complexion, which became delicately pink at the top of the cheeks, as if burning tears had left their attenuated trace there.

In him the passionate aptitudes were betrayed by the elegance of the flexible neck and the almost excessive but ideally harmonious slenderness of a body that one divined to be robust beneath the docile pleats of his garments.

If happiness—that blue bird—is a rare species, one thought nevertheless on seeing them, that it exists; and perhaps destiny cannot be reckoned an enemy without injustice, since it sometimes permits the encounter of two such individuals, who are for one another, fatally, an inexhaustible source of more-than-human delights.

At the end of the Canebière, wallowing in the sunlight like a beautiful ruminating beast, the port puts over the sky a suggestive grimoire of complicated and delicate masts, which, for the eyes of lovers, signifies the intoxication of distant voyages and free happiness under the free sky.

The temptation of an excursion at sea becomes irresistible.

✳

Sitting at the rear of the boat, they now have the perfect illusion of solitude in the middle of the sumptuous Mediterranean, the queen with a blue mantle to whom the infatuated sky brings colors.

The old matelot maneuvering the oars gives the impression of being made of wood, like the boat, and does not embarrass their intimacy at all.

They are holding hands, and from the ships at anchor an intense and exciting desire comes to them for departures toward the unknown and magnetic distance.

Alas, with a groan, the lover has made his counterpart
a somber confession: he is married.

"But see, dear soul, these vessels, these propitious
vessels with sails woven of hope. Oh, let's go far away
together, further than memories and the tyranny of
the accomplished fact, to the marvelous land called
Elsewhere."

Berthe, sobbing quietly, responds: "Yes, let's depart.
Where you go, I will go."

Their cabin is retained aboard the *Orénoque*, which is
sailing in three days, and they return to their room delectably weary.

As Berthe drops her gloves on to the table she perceives the letter that she wrote that morning and forgot,
her letter to Germaine. Would you like, dearest, to put
this in the post immediately, in order that I can obtain a
reply before our departure.

He responds by putting his arm round the pretty
waist leaning over the table and puts little kisses in the
fine hair, while Berthe writes before her lover's eyes, who
follows it without intending to do so:

Madame Germaine de Lohan, aux Aulnaies, near Lyon

Suddenly, he draws away, troubled and going pale,
and says in a voice that has become singular:

"Oh, Lord God! You know my wife, then?"

PARDONED

To Monsieur Camille de Sainte-Croix.[1]

HIS decision is made. He will marry the pretty Juliette, who possesses for all her wealth under the sun a pair of dark eyes worth all the diamonds in Brazil, and the grace of a queen of flowers, in her modest woolen dresses.

Oh, they will not be very rich, for he has only a modest position as a teacher and a book of beautiful verses in the loft of a publisher who respects himself too much to "launch" an unknown.

But the eternal history of Amour making an upholsterer, maître d'hôtel, carter and ordinary supplier of Their Majesties the Amorous will be true once again.

Will they not find, in fact, in their nest furnished on credit, the joyous luxury of magical palaces? And what idleness on the cushions of coupés would be worth the

---

1 The journalist and novelist Camille de Sainte-Croix (1859-1915) was a member of the Hydropathes and habitué of the Chat Noir, along with Krysinska, in the 1880s. He also published in *L'Écho de Paris*.

sweet lassitude of returns, arm in arm, from walks that have been expressly made very distant?

And then, there would be the charming repose, during the vacations, with the dear old woman in the Pyrenees, the mother who remained something of a peasant, slightly puritanical and slightly intolerant, but so proud of her boy in Paris: a poet whom everyone admired.

Fernand Colzy even had the firm intention of imposing a patient silence on his flesh, crying out for amour toward the admirable prey that almost offered itself, by virtue of confident abandon and also of tenderness.

But, one evening at the end of winter, as they were returning from a distant excursion in the air already perfumed by the sly renewal of things that remain, when we pass so rapidly, in the almost religious fear of seeing the excessively rapid hours flee, they took one another avidly.

There was then an amorous piracy, a pillage of kisses, of furious and indefatigable embraces.

Fernand asked for a leave from his school, furnished a certificate from his friend, the physician Bougarès, who declared that he was ill and was scarcely lying, for lovesickness had the cloud-embracing poet firmly in its grip. But this time the clouds were living nacre; it was an entire sky that he held in his arms and an entire harvest of dreams hatching under the most fulgurant suns that he devoured on breasts as roseate as mornings, in arms as luminous as moonlight.

Juliette's black hair had the musky fragrance of precious furs, and flowed heavily over her back like a river of black wine carrying irrational desires.

Doubtless passionate atavisms were dormant in the rich blood of the young man, for, as soon as her virgin fears had been vanquished, she became the ardent and savant accomplice of the poet with the profile of a faun, whose friends remember him today with a faithful and melancholy tenderness.

For eight months there was a joyful, Sardanapalesque dilapidation of all living forces. The calms, although delectable, seemed to them to be sacrileges against the dear and implacable God who possessed them and was killing them.

The first repose dated from the day when the physician declared his friend gravely afflicted and said to Fernand, with the vibrant and harsh accent of their common homeland: "You're doomed if you don't escape to the Pyrenees right away." And he added: "Without her, of course."

"He's an imbecile," said Fernand, when his excellent friend had gone. "You'll come with me, darling, won't you? And we'll come back married."

During the journey, the poor amorous woman thought she could see her friend expiring. The beautiful eyes of burnished gold, which she had seen illuminated by the brilliant torches of Eros, in the hours of ecstasy, were burning now as funereal lamps with the fire of imminent death.

But when, after an atrocious night passed in a railway carriage, dawn rose over the beautiful green mountains, rejoiced by vine plants climbing the hills; when the nascent daylight had caressed with rosy reflections the gray and delicately mossy rocks that alternated with the cultivated heights, Fernand felt better so suddenly that it seemed a miracle.

A miracle: yes, it needed nothing less than that to save the poet. But there are no more miracles, because we no longer believe in them.

A week after arriving in his homeland, Fernand, bed-ridden, knew that he was dying: slowly and laboriously, with cruel alternations of recovered health, deceptive respites . . .

Juliette, mad with grief, cared for him like a little child, keeping vigil night and day next to the bed of suffering.

And the already heavy eyelids of the moribund, the eyelids oppressed by delirious hauntings, sometimes opened under the refreshing rain of tears shed by the friend.

Out there in Bordes, the entire region trembled with execration against "the Parisienne." On the very day of her arrival Fernand had almost been shoved out of the door by his mother, although he was her unique pride and joy. The hatred of the reproving old woman against "the other" was so strong that the beloved son was ex-pelled from the hearth because of the contact by which he had been irredeemably soiled.

"Oh, the wretch! The Parisienne!" barked the poor mother, when Fernand had departed to install himself in Castex, higher up, in order to die. "The whore! Look what she's made of my boy! A corpse! And also a pagan, who lives with a woman as if the holy sacrament of mar-riage were made for dogs! Oh, a bitch herself . . ."

La Cagarel, an old peasant woman, brought provisions to the accursed household "up there" every morning.

And every morning, when she came down, the mother seized her furiously, demanding news. Then, throughout the rest of the day, there were vehement commentaries in the village.

Perdigail, Lozerin and Gouragne, the elders, chatted gathered in the farmhouse, their voluble pipes in their teeth.

"One can see that she's nothing much just by her gloves; would an honest woman have gloves up to the elbows?"

"Of course, that's the outfit of a kept woman."

"Yes, who reeks like a church."

"And those eyes of perdition!"

"Oh, the horror!"

"Poor Fernand!"

"Such a brave poet."

The women contented themselves with blushing and lowering their eyes if anyone mentioned Fernand's name, as if it were a bad word.

One day, old Cagarel came down with red eyes, for having wept. Madame Colzy, on seeing her, did not question her again, but went frightfully pale and vacillated on her legs, like a drunkard.

Up there, Fernand was in his death-throes.

It was the tender, almost seductive death of consumptives, a pitiful delirium veiling the mists of his brain, harassed by insomnia.

A terrible blow of a fist on the door made Juliette, collapsed on her knees, jump.

When she had opened it she recoiled with a cry.

It was the mother.

The old puritan threw herself into Juliette's arms, racked by sobs, moaning: "You've loved him bravely, at least . . . loved bravely . . . !"

Fernand, now, in a plaintive voice, was reciting prayers, first in French, then in Latin, as when he was a child in the choir, and then in French again.

"Our Father, who art in Heaven . . ."

Verses also, sonorous strophes, caressed and reheated by all his vigorous amour, all his passion for the Beautiful, of which he was now dying. Then prayers again.

"Hallowed be thy name, thy kingdom come . . ."

The mother and the young woman were kneeling by the bed, holding hands, when the priest came—too late.

Three days later the same carriage took Juliette and Madame Colzy to Bordes, where Fernand was to be buried.

Placing a hand on her shoulder, the old woman said to the young one: "Since you're leaving tomorrow, at least spend the night in the house."

"Thank you, oh, thank you!" Juliette sobbed. "How good you are! But I dare not . . . I can't . . ."

"What I'm telling you," the poor mother wept, very timidly, "is that at least you won't be troubled . . . the whole country is against you . . . they loved our Fernand so much . . . they were so proud of him . . . someone might perhaps cause you annoyance."

At that moment the carriage, half way to Bordes, made a detour and fell into a compact mass of people weeping loudly, with childish and incoherent chants of chagrin.

"Let's at least see her!"

"Where is she, Fernand's darling?"

The carriage was stopped, and women, climbing on to the footstep, kissed Juliette.

Men also came to rub their rough beards against the young woman's hands.

Was Juliette not the relic left by the dear departed, something that had belonged to him intimately, who had had all his amour, shared his last minutes . . . ?

"Come to our house for the night."

"No, to ours."

"To ours, rather."

They were not far from brawling when Madame Colzy declared, harshly: "She isn't going with any of you, worthy folk; she's coming to my house, since she's like my daughter, isn't that so?"

A HONEYMOON VOYAGE

To M. Philippe Gille.[1]

THE hrabia[2] Jean and his young wife Ludga are sitting on the two sides of the window of a first-class compartment, entirely given to the joy of having been able to take the two corners coveted by travelers. But now that the train has moved off, after the automatic whistle of the signal, without producing an influx of people, their joy becomes almost boundless in having that little domicile cutting through space all to themselves.

After the bustle of trunks to pack, crocodile tears to wipe away between the stifling arms of friends, the anguish caused by the treason of dressmakers and all the other tribulations before the departure, they can dream at last!

It is not a rerun in reverse of their brief romance that is in their minds, but disconnected evocations.

Ludga sees again the white and gold room where, quivering like a sparrow dying in the snow, she had the

---

1 The dramatist and librettist Philippe Gille (1831-1901) was another supporter of Krysinska's claim to be the pioneer of *vers libre*.
2 Author's note: "Title of Slav nobility."

revelation of her femininity in the powerful and gentle arms of the Beloved. A dazzlement full of terrors and delights. Her memory fits that complex sensation of similitudes with a heroic Fanfare, in which, amid the implacable sonorousness of brass instruments, swooning violins are weeping.

He remembers the walk in Prince R***'s park, after the tea when he said so many stupid things and Ludga, for the first time, leaned on his arm. The stars vacillated in the depths of the pure cold sky like pious flames in the crystal of a lamp, and merely by the manner in which the light falling from the star on her tresses soaked them like tears, he saw that she held his life in her little hand, which, that evening, for the first time, was supported by his arm.

She had scarcely changed since. Only, her tresses, then assiduous companions of her virginal shoulders, now rose up like golden flames springing from her nape and taking refuge under the hood that she has adopted precisely in order to give the impression of a married lady.

The northern country, all plains—infinite grasslands like green skies, where flocks wander like clouds under the soft gray sky above, grazed by errant clouds—are drowned in shadow and silence, brutally punctuated by the jolts of the train.

Two nights and two days had passed on the railway when they arrived in Paris, familiar to both of them, so they only spent one unquiet night there in a hotel with corridors as noisy as the streets, and the impatience to see the Midi sat them down again in a carriage.

The Midi! They were going to surprise the Midi in its lair! And the southerners! They expected, to begin with, a picture postcard landscape full of the sly and gracious affectation of romance, devoid of any character.

And the people! Oh, my friends, the gesticulations they were going to see! And turning the tap of talk in order not to say anything.

They were passing now through the Bourbonnais, and marveled at seeing wine—bought so dearly in their country—casually climbing the hills, which, dotted with stakes, resembled green brushes destined for the hair of a god.

As they approached the Auvergne, the vines were unbound and, free, seemed to be dancing the ancient dances of the Bacchantes, or crawling, drunk on their own sap, and lying down for Olympia slumbers. The soil was humped by the backs of peaceful animals where the grass grew without hindrance. The mauve sails of the highest mountains appeared on the horizon.

They were able to descend at Clermont-Ferrand for dinner and embark again on the train that would leave them in Marseille the next morning. The compartment was crammed with passengers. At the stations some got down, and all that remained was one family and household going to Montpellier, a fortunate city that had seen them born. The family consisted of an old woman as meager and brown as a prune who was telling her rosary beads, her daughter and her son-in-law, who were already asleep, mouths open, with the idiotic air of dead fish.

Jean and Ludga did not take long to learn all that without there being the slightest need for diplomacy to obtain that result. They were also informed that the daughter's name was Isabelle, that the movement of the train discomfited her and made her seasick, as well as the old woman. They did not know how long it would take to get there, and it would soon be something else entirely on that horrible line, which was the only line in the world as bad.

The hrabia and his wife, alarmed, wanted to try another compartment, but they were all packed, so they returned to their places, heartbroken.

The train followed the slopes of mountains and swayed like a bear, continually going into long tunnels, the cold air of which it cleaved with a thunderous rumble reverberated by the vault. The mother and the daughter had taken possession of the two windows, where they went to retch every two minutes and then issued bulletins on their health to the whole compartment

"Oh, good! That's better, I've unloaded my stomach."

It was commencing, the Midi; it commenced so well that Jean and Ludga were not far from having had enough of it. The household from Montpellier had a little more decency. The man had taken off his shoes in order to put on slippers, and, coiffed in a fez, he stretched out on one of the banquettes and did not stop snoring until Nîmes.

Jean and Ludga, besieged in the worst places, were near to weeping. There was no point in thinking about sleep. The son-in-law of the old woman continually took an enormous valise from the net above their heads, saying: "A thousand pardons" and made distributions to the two women of slices of lemon, ether on sugar-lumps and little glasses of Chartreuse to help them feel better. Finally, at Nîmes, they changed lines; the hrabia and his wife, left alone, were able to sleep a little.

At about five o'clock in the morning, Jean woke Ludga, who looked out of the window and uttered a cry. The tragic plains of the Crau were ripened by the rocks looming up like demons, and oppressing the ground beneath the weight of their hostile meditation, where, among the stones as bright as bones, rare plaintive and lunar green olive trees wept, with mad fearful gestures. Up above far away—too high and too far—was a steely sky decorated with victorious crimsons by the rising sun. It was as beautiful as suicide.

The train, launched at full speed, was engulfed in tunnels and quarries, vomiting noise, seemingly devouring the stones and chewing them noisily.

When the landscape reappeared, there were further landslides of livid rocks, which, in the increasing vertiginousness of the train, gave the impression of falling, like a flock of evil eagles, on the consternated country, the heaths without hope of wheat. There were no more olive trees; only tenacious fig trees with hard leaves varnished with metallic gleams extended their arms.

Ludga, her eyes harassed by that course through the abyss, was huddled in her corner; her little feet climbed up like two mice on to the cushion where, facing her, her husband was sitting. She said: "But where do they go in search of their ballads, their farces and their proverbial gaiety?"

"All the gaieties are proverbial, my beauty, and there is, in fact, nothing at which to laugh or about which to sing ballads in the Midi; it's simply very beautiful, very wild and full of character—but only northern artists can see that, because they're the only ones who look. The southerner—mediocre, of course—doesn't look. He has no need to look; he divines. He has too much genius, and that prevents him from having talent."

"Oh, it doesn't give me the slightest desire to sing, to the tune of Monsieur Thomas: 'Do you know the land where the orange tree flowers?'"[1]

"It's certainly better than that, the land of orange trees: as sad and accursed as Sin, as beautiful as Despair, under a glorious sky, like Pardon."

They were approaching Marseille, and the landscape became somewhat domesticated. Eucalypti bordered the road and plantations of olives, pruned for the cultivation of the fruit, made one think of a primitive and resigned life. The sun, at the zenith, allowed light to diffuse in the diaphanous firmament as if through the globe of an unpolished blue crystal lamp.

Their sojourn in Marseille was a new astonishment. The elegant city was traversed with bonhomie by wide, populous and busy boulevards, markets full of flowers, fruits and watermelons in heaps on the ground, and beautiful sturdy young women carrying enormous heavy

---

1 The reference is to a song from Ambroise Thomas's comic opera *Mignon* (1866), based on J. W. Goethe's *Wilhelm Meisters Lehrjahre*.

baskets on their heads in the ancient fashion, and finally, the Canebière, as splendid and fresh as Alhambras, where courteous, discreet and soberly gesturing people came to sit down.

"Our Midi has been changed into a nurse," said Ludga to her husband, laughing, as they boarded a train to go to Monte Carlo.

❋

The hrabia and his wife had lunch on the terrace of the Hôtel de Paris. Having arrived in Monte Carlo the day before, they intended to spend one or two days there before departing for Italy. That morning, Ludga was wearing a very straight gray silk dress that made the gold of her camellia complexion vibrate. Like the wings of seagulls over the waves of a placid ocean, her eyelashes palpitated over her large gray eyes, which shone with an exotic warmth, slightly brutal for her northern blood, and perhaps a hint of curious impatience dieted toward the white palace visible from there: the Casino.

❋

The gaming room: the three roulette tables are three packets of black and silent crowd, from which the susurrus emerges of shifting gold, adding further to the imposing impression of a swarm of flies gathering over some flavorsome prey.

Jean and Ludga stroll through the hall, observing that it is not very interesting. Everything that is spoken by the expressive physiognomy of the gambler is a bad joke. When, through a gap, they can perceive faces, they see a kind of gathering of faithful sectarians, exclusively devoted to the cult of Indifference. It is like a temple of atony and the death of nerves, which would not resist if they were alive, being broken, like the strings of mishandled musical instruments.

The hrabia and his wife have drawn closer together; the gambling is beginning to amuse them slightly. The roulette wheel rotates with the click of a macabre dreary round dance in which little kneecaps are colliding.

Ludga says: "It's necessary only to bet on the color that has passed once; hazard being picturesque, one has only the most improbable thing against it: perfect symmetry—which is to say, intermittence. Do you want me to try?"

She puts a hundred francs on red, which wins. She cannot forbid herself a sadness as she picks up the two banknotes. What if she had bet a thousand francs? Her victory of a pretty calculator would have been greater. Then, it is like losing nine hundred francs rather than winning. The following spin is black; she has not bet, but for the next one, she deliberately takes out a thousand francs, which she bets on black. It is red, and the thousand francs are lost.

Well, it is a little vexing, but she continues her system and puts a thousand francs on red.

"Eleven, black, odd and low," announces the croupier.

Ludga feels herself stung, like a little whiplash on her eyelids, and demands her husband's wallet with a masculine abruptness that he does not recognize. She almost snatches it from his hands, irritated by his slowness, and puts two thousand-franc bills on black, one of which tears in her hand, which is beginning to tremble.

"Twenty-two, red, odd and high."

"That's too much," murmurs Ludga. "Absolute intermittence, the absurdity . . ."

The piles of gold, overturned and swept away by the rake, render a sound similar to that made by surgical instruments moved prior to an operation.

Ludga, with blood in her cheeks, puts a thousand francs on twenty-two. Twenty-two comes up and she has won thirty-five thousand francs. A happy as a little girl at having succeeded with an audacious coup, she seizes her husband's arm almost brutally and drags him toward the exit.

But Jean is sad. He has never seen Ludga so passionate. Is it possible that she is avaricious, that angel?

Before them, the sea opens its vast blue eyes, as tender and implacable as a child's eyes. All of the rigid and hostile vegetation is bristling against humans; the palms are cut out of metal and the gray-green aloes resemble caimans coming to the water's edge to open their long jaws, yawning with ennui.

Ludga sees the white laurels disappearing under flowers like a snow of stars, and the mimosas with odorous yellow pearls. In the silence of the park where they are walking—also silently—only the melancholy cooing coming from the aviary of pigeons irritates them both. Finally obsessed, they decide to go and sit down at the Café de Paris. There, they only observe the sinister heads of people horrified by living, faces holed by eyes devoid of gazes, with eyelids violet with fever, like twin bruises, which the sun inconveniences with its great honest light. Very correct gentlemen are meditating before their coffee cups like Socrates condemned to drink the hemlock.

Ludga is bored. She dare not confess that she is dying of the desire to return to the gaming table. She ends up admitting it to her husband, who consents immediately, by virtue of a mysterious perversity, for he is truly suffering.

"Be prudent, my dear," says Jean, without really knowing what he is saying, as they climb the shiny stairway. But Ludga is immediately offended. Has she not won, and can he not have confidence in her? The idea comes to her to cover herself with glory by means of a bold coup. She puts the maximum on red, as much on even and as much on high.

"Eleven, black, odd and low." That is eighteen thousand francs lost at a single stroke. Her throat literally dry, she repeats the same bet, and loses again.

"You're playing like a fool," said Jean, with a voice that has become strange. "Let me do it." And, snatching the wallet from her hand, he lays a bet.

Ludga, wounded in the heart, horribly unhappy, prays to Heaven that he loses everything. But he does not lose. He even bets on the numbers that come up, and realizes, in half an hour, a profit of nearly a hundred thousand francs.

Ludga remarks in the meantime, an artery in his temple that leaps like a frog, and she finds it infinitely ridiculous. So that man, so handsome, so noble, whom she idolizes with such an absolute fervor, is as passionate about money as a horse-trader. He no longer even spares a glance for her. So much the better, for she is horrified by him. He is losing again now, and finds himself at odds. At that point, the folly ends and he draws his wife out of the hall.

Without even discussing it, they return to the hotel to give orders for the departure. But they do not continue their voyage; they are weary. They return to the white and cold land of Poland, with something irremediable between them, for having picked the bitter fruit of the Tree of Knowledge and gazed into the depths of their souls, which are like the beautiful waves of the Mediterranean, reflecting on the surface of the vast sky of God but rolling monsters and the cadavers of monsters in the depths.

A *FIN-DE-SIÈCLE* MIDNIGHT SUPPER

To George Auriol[1]

"MONSIEUR CHÉRIN, if you please?"
"Third floor to the left, number eighteen."
Young Léo had decided, for the first time, to come to the room of the student who has been courting her for several weeks without any success . . . of esteem.

She brought with her Antoinette, newly arrived from Chartres to study at the Maternité, and who, in the meantime, was allowing herself to be shown around the Latin Quarter, playfully, by Léo, a childhood friend who had "turned out badly" according to friends and relatives in Chartres, and who was "making her way" according to her dressmaker in Paris.

---

1 George Auriol was the signature used by the poet, songwriter and pioneer of Art Nouveau baptized Jean-George Huyot (1863-1938), whose name remains familiar because of the font of type named after him. He was an habitué of the Chat Noir alongside Krysinska. It is not obvious why his name is not preceded by the honorific "M." like the majority of the dedicatees.

In any case, the escapade was inoffensive: a midnight supper of young people, that was all.

There would be crepes and witty remarks; they would break the back of a terrine of *foie gras*; they would open a few bottles of champagne, and speak ill of their neighbors, which was better than saying stupid things.

In sum, they would amuse themselves enormously.

And after all, if the champagne turned out to be a perfidious counselor . . .

As Antoinette, a charming brunette of nineteen, stood outside the door, emotionally, without daring to knock, Mademoiselle Léo called her squarely a silly goose.

Antoinette, who had read Mürger and Alfred de Musset, was quite bewildered on going into room number eighteen. Young but grave gentlemen, dressed better than embassy attachés on duty and almost as well as bookmakers, were sitting down around a table and playing cards phlegmatically.

Several women—the mistresses of those messieurs—having retired to a divan, were jabbering concierge French with spoiled voices, while their hands, in gloves with fourteen buttons, rolled cigarettes.

The arrival of Léo and Antoinette did not disturb anyone. None of the card-players stood up. Only Monsieur Chérin said: "Bonjour, Princesses. Messieurs, I introduce these ladies to you."

From the gaming table, illuminated by four candles, sibylline syllables emerged:

"*Banco à cheval.*"

"I fold."

"I double."

"No more bets."

Meanwhile, Léo, in a whisper, introduced Monsieur Chérin's comrades to her friend

"The tall dark-haired fellow with a lorgnon is Monsieur Valu, a law student like Chérin, a very chic type. The tall blond with the monocle is Monsieur Léon Méral, the 'husband' of Madame Blanche."

Madame Blanche acquiesced with a majestic nod of the head. She had light chestnut hair, the eyes of a boiled turbot and a somnolent distinction caused by morphine injections.

"The one lighting his cigar there at the end of the table, with a coachman's waistcoat, is a Romanian, the son of a family who has become a horse-trader by taste. He's with Madame Bébé, whom I introduce to you."

Madame Bébé, who was concluding an anecdote of the time she was a waitress in the Chien Savant brasserie, experienced the need to make some ostentatious gesture; she traversed the room deliberately, her hands in the pockets of her tailored green jacket, approached the gaming table and said: "I'll play. Banker, a louis to drop."

It was a flop. Women were not allowed to play. The Rumanian said: "Leave us in peace, will you. We're here to enjoy ourselves."

The clock, an Eiffel Tower in simulated cast iron, marked half past midnight: an hour more than solemn.

Then the ladies rebelled.

"Enough gambling like that. We're hungry."

Monsieur Chérin rang for the house waiter.

"What do you have to eat?"

"Nothing, Monsieur . . . but there's the charcuterie in the Boulevard Saint-Michel. I'll go and fetch whatever Monsieur wishes."

Madame Bébé made a list of victuals.

"Aren't we going to have crepes?" advanced Antoinette, timidly.

They rang for the waiter again. "Try to find some crepes."

"Yes, Monsieur."

But he came back without crepes. It would have been necessary to go further, all the way to the Rue Dauphine.

And the little feast commenced.

The women ate alone.

"We'll have finished in ten minutes and we'll be all yours," Chérin had said.

But they never finished, and they were dying of hunger.

Smoked tongues, washed down with an apocryphal Bordeaux, appeased that of the ladies, doubtless by virtue of a sympathetic effect.

Blanche, in the voice of a hoarse seraph, told the story of her miscarriage, with technical terms and a joyful luxury of details.

Madame Bébé thought she ought to protest and indicated that, with a wink, to the little one, who was listening, astounded. But she earned a rebuke.

"You must truly be stupid, my dear, to take exception to that; it's science."

"Pass us a few sandwiches, then," cried someone at the gaming table.

"Come and sup with us instead."

"In a minute. We're finishing the deal."

For a few minutes, Antoinette's charming dark eyes had been fixed, fascinated, on the tall Valu. The young provincial's admiration went toward that elegant fellow—a delicate and intelligent admiration, with something more tender. She took him a sandwich, coquettishly, on the lid of a box of bonbons.

"Thank you, dear child!" he said, without looking at her, as he picked up his cards, which were superb: the nine of hearts and the queen of spades.

The Eiffel Tower now marked two o'clock. The young men were still playing cards.

In order to break the somnolence that was beginning to overtake the feminine contingent, Madame Bébé said: "Sing us something, little one . . . you must have a pretty voice."

And, accompanied by the vague tapping of Léo on an out-of-tune piano. Antoinette sang:

> *I didn't think about Rose*
> *Rose came with me to the wood.*
> *We talked about this and that.*
> *I no longer remember what.*

I was fifteen and morose,
She was twenty; her eyes shone
The nightingales sang Rose,
And the blackbirds whistled me.[1]

Between the admirable lines of the master, the musician had inserted the rumor of branches populated with amorous birds, and Antoinette's young voice sang like bright waterfalls.

The tall Valu had definitely made the conquest of that little heart, which gave itself thus, in the caressing and appealing voice of an amorous turtle-dove.

I only saw that she was beautiful
When, emerging from the wood
She said: "Don't give it another thought."
Since when, I've thought of nothing else.

Valu was holding the bank at that moment and losing heavily. The Rumanian was trying hard to break it, desirous of dealing himself.

"Shut the piano, Mesdames, I beg you," cried Valu, his nerves martyrized by the anguish of a decisive coup.

That was too much for poor Antoinette, who burst into sobs and collapsed in an attack of nerves.

Aided by Léo, Madame Bébé, who was as strong as a horse, carried her to Chérin's bed, where the little one be-

---

1 The words are those of a poem by Victor Hugo, published in *Contemplations* (1856); it was probably one of those set to music by Krysinska.

gan to calm down at the compassionate contact of those female hands, which undid her blouse and moistened the temples with Eau de Lubin.

The game, momentarily interrupted, resumed, and Valu, who was winning a little money back, said: "She's hysterical, that child. Another subject for Charcot."

NORETTE

To M. Charles Chincholle.[1]

AT the end of the good dinner at Uncle Bujat's, where nothing had been forgotten that could expand the little tubes and render the nerves happy and slack, Félix Guimau, decidedly overtaken, recognized that the time had come to "despoil the old man" and establish himself by marrying his cousin.

He made the proposal immediately to his uncle, a first-class pharmacist positioned at one of the best street corners, with a triumphant pair of huge bottles aimed, like the eyes of a wolf, at the quarter.

The chandelier, charged with chains like a convict, flooded the tablecloth, which seemed to be burning, with a heavy light, filled the spoons and liqueur glasses with fire, put a zinc plaque on the black satin corsage molding the opulent bosom of Aunt Bujat, padded Monsieur Bujat's baldness with gold and then went to varnish the reliefs of the sculpted sideboard.

---

1 Charles Chincholle (1843-1902) worked for André Dumas before establishing himself as one of the foremost journalists of his day.

Félix was melting with bliss and applauded himself for having finally made a decision, with the exaggeration of enthusiasm that one deploys when one wants absolutely to persuade oneself that everything is for the best.

His cousin Julienne was certainly not pretty, with her head of a fat young sheep and her limp hair, which offered specimens of all the blondes, from the gray blonde of carpentry wood to the red blonde of tanned leather.

And then, what would Norette say?

He saw again the pretty brunette who had been living by his side for four years like a good little wife.

But his resolution was made. He was a man of resolution, damn it! It seemed to him that that ought to explain everything.

"What are you thinking about—the death of Louis XVI?" said Uncle Bujat.

That was the first-class pharmacist's customary joke, every time anyone permitted himself in his presence the incongruity of seeming to be thinking about something.

Julienne laughed, as was the custom when Papa made a joke—which is to say that she exposed to examination the majority of her teeth, while her eyes, having remained serious, confessed that she was not amused as all that.

"You know," Félix ended up saying, "I'm not bored with you, but it's a long way to Neuilly, and it's getting late."

"Good, good, don't stand on ceremony with us," the chorus replied, and the uncle added: "You can kiss your cousin."

Félix approached Julienne, who turned her head away with so much modesty that instead of a kiss on the cheek he took one close to the ear, pulling out a few hairs of the turquoise forget-me-not moustache that ornamented the lobe.

✳

Félix was not really at ease on returning to Neuilly, to his florist/pharmacist's shop, which communicated with the room where Norette had gone to sleep while waiting for him.

From her open hand, the novel of *Monte Cristo* had slid on to the bedside rug, and that hand, of an ingenuous model, fallen on to the coverlet, gave the impression of a tulip shedding its petals in the atmosphere saturated with good perfumes of clean linen and essences poured into water. Under the lampshade, Norette was sleeping the profound slumber that young health provides. Her skin took on a luster of vellum, stretched over the firm plumpness of her shoulders of a vigorous Berrichonne who did not refuse herself anything good. That was clearly visible in her greedy lips, liberally parted, and the supple and vivid line of the nose, graciously protrusive between the eyes, where the eyelids with lowered lashes put a little veil of shadow.

For a long time, Félix watched the young woman sleeping who had made his life tender and warm, since he had lost his mother—a loss that had caused him such a rude chagrin that he had failed his end of year examination and had not been sober for a month.

Oh, if only one could have Uncle Bujat's pharmacy *and* Norette!

But that was a dream, and it was not a matter of dreaming but of being energetic and furnishing his career honorably. As for Norette, a fate would be made for her; she would be established, and one day, she would be able to marry some honest fellow who would make her happy.

At that sequence of future prospects Félix grimaced, as if he had had to swallow the most abominable drug in the Bujat pharmacy. But he was determined.

Norette had woken up, with the pretty awakening of a child, her fists in her eyes, and Félix told himself that this was the moment, or never, to finish it with an inevitable scene.

"You know, darling, there's news, and news that won't amuse you—nor me, either, in fact."

"What? What is it?"

"It's that, in two months, I'm going to marry my cousin; but you'd be wrong to be jealous, for there's nothing to be jealous of, certainly not, nothing at all."

Norette, caught on the hop, was unable to make any scene; but as the convinced tone of that finale calmed her chagrin slightly, she burst into noisy sobs.

"Come on, darling," said Félix, who was beginning to lose his head, "be reasonable; you don't want to make me lose my career; you know that one can't do what one wishes. If it weren't a matter of very serious things"—he could see the two superb bottles—"would I ever quit my Norette, whom I love?"

He sat down on the bed, wrapping his arms around the young woman shaken by sobs, and put heart-broken little kisses on her shoulders and breasts, moistened by warm tears.

"What will become of me?" Norette lamented.

"What will become of you? Oh, you can't believe me to be wicked enough to leave my darling in difficulty. I'll install you in a nice little dress shop, where you'll be like a queen."

"I'll be the boss?" Norette began to say, smiling through her tears, half-consoled.

"Yes, you'll be the boss, and it will be written over the shop in golden letters: *Mademoiselle Norette.*"

"No, Madame Norette, that's more serious,"

"And more exact," added Félix, cheerfully, proud of having possessed the pretty future boss all to himself for four years.

The next day, nothing of the storms of the previous night appeared. Norette ran the four quarters of Pars in search of a shop for hire. Félix sold his drugs to the rare clients of Neuilly, while awaiting the glories of the Bujat pharmacy.

Three times a week he went to pay his court to his cousin, and the rest of the time he delivered himself to amorous delights in the arms of his mistress, spiced and exacerbated by the dolor of an imminent separation.

That had lasted a month when one day, Norette gave him some consternating news: she was pregnant.

"Oh well, oh well," repeated Félix, bewildered, as she stood directly before him, her eyes ringed, with her corset undone beneath her peignoir. "There's a poor little thing who'll arrive like March in Lent."

"Yes, you can say that, like March in Lent."

"But what can we do?"

"Yes, what can we do?" the woman repeated, like an echo.

"An abortion is dangerous."

"Oh, it's dangerous?"

"Yes, but it's done thousands of times and people come out of it very well."

Without losing a minute—he was definitely a man of resolution—Félix went to get some ergot-infested rye from his pharmacy,[1] which he dosed copiously, for the girl was sturdy, and he couldn't miss the trick; the child would have spoiled all their plans.

Norette accepted the drug without difficulty. She had already found a delightful shop, and was infatuated with her future life as a boss; it was truly no time to encumber herself with a fatherless brat.

Slightly feverish, Félix went downstairs to serve his clients. When he went back up for dinner he was nailed to the floor outside the door by profound groans. He went in, intoxicated by anguish, and ran to the bed where Norette was writhing in the final convulsions of death by poisoning. Félix Guimau had done things too well; the dose had been too strong, and the mother was dying with the child.

As she fell back on the cushions, her hands arrested in the clawing of the terminal agony, he repeated, stupidly: "God of God! God of God! This is stupid! God of God!"

And he burst into sobs, fell to the floor next to the bed, like a brute, and remained there all evening and

---

1 Ergot was first popularized as an abortifacient in the early nineteenth century and marketed in pill form by numerous pharmaceutical companies in the early twentieth century, in various euphemistic guises.

all night; he ended up going to sleep, emptied of tears and emptied of the horror of his thoughts, and even the capacity for suffering.

✳

He woke up the next morning at the usual time, and strove for some time to doubt that the catastrophe was a *fait accompli* rather than an odious nightmare from which he would soon emerge. But the rejected certainty entered and fulgurated like a cruel dawn, like a dawn of distress, and was amplified by an obsession: what if someone discovered the thing? What would become of him then?

And Fear dragged him by the hair in the midst of howling crowds to where the scaffold stood, with the sinister flash of the blade.

Six o'clock chimed.

That was the moment when Norette usually made the coffee, crouched next to the little stove, bright in her hastily-knotted skirts, her breasts free under the chemise crumpled by the night. And it was already an avid pleasure to see her, arms bare, pouring boiling water into the filter, slowly, with the attentive gaze of her eyes, which resembled two large drops of coffee, while the exquisite perfume filled the room, seeming to emanate from her brown skin.

The black stove, and the thought that the coffee would not be made, absorbed all his faculties of suffering momentarily. Then Fear returned again.

He bathed his face in water, put a comb through his hair in order to give the impression of doing what he did every day, and went down to open the shop.

Clients succeeded one another: regulars who lingered for a little chat, housewives who never finished explaining their case: "It's a cramp in the stomach, so, something to put me right again."

Very amiably, he listened patiently, advised inoffensive things, surprising himself by admiring himself at times for that perfect act.

The terrible thing was when he found himself alone. Then he went mad again, wondering whether he might not do better to flee. But where?

New arrivals of clients restored his aplomb. He felt surges of gratitude and affection toward every human face that placed itself between him and his intimate torture.

Night came, invading the bleak enclosures of the properties visible through the window: a line of sad and suspicious walls, isolating comfortable existences alongside the deserted causeway.

Hunger was now gnawing his entrails, but he dared not go anywhere for fear of being noticed.

When his shop was closed he went to buy bread, and returned to devour it in the room where the young woman was sleeping forever—with her eyes open.

As soon as his meal had been swallowed, a despotic lassitude overwhelmed him, plunging him into a sudden slumber, his nose on the table. But the cold woke him up, the cold of the first nights of autumn, and then the chill of fever in the marrowbones, which made his teeth chatter and bound him as if in excessively tight clothes soaked in icy water. Mechanically, he undressed, no longer remembering, wanting to go to bed.

As he was about to climb into the bed he encountered the eyes of the dead woman, where the pale light of the stars was stagnating, as if reflected by dormant waters. He recoiled with a whimper of horror. Awakened completely this time, he dressed again with the shaky hands of an old man.

To flee, to flee . . . no matter where . . . but to flee!

He left the house, locking the door, and went to wander in silent and deserted Neuilly, walking in the middle of a wide causeway bordered on both sides by the walls of enclosures, black and similar.

He wandered all night, but in the morning, instinctively, he returned to the shop and served the clients until the evening, as usual, sensing that salvation, however distantly possible it might be, was at that price.

And it was necessary to finish with that situation of damnation—but how? How?

Having gone up to the bedroom again he paced back and forth with long strides. He bumped into the bed, which rendered a groan, and made him flee to the far end of the room, mad with fear.

A hatred came to him for that cadaver. He had always had a presentiment that that woman would doom him. They never do anything else, women.

Deep down, however, a rudiment of hope lurked. Norette, an orphan, had no one who could enquire about her disappearance.

Oh, if he could only find a means of sending back into oblivion, into propitious and paternal Annihilation, the terrible *thing* that was his beloved mistress.

Memories of celebrated crimes haunted him: women cut into pieces, cadavers boiled in vats, calcined in furnaces, expedited in crates to distant destinations.

Yes, but all that ended up being discovered!

And again, apparitions of the scaffold strangled him with fear.

He suddenly remembered that it was the evening when he was expected at Uncle Bujat's

That appeared to him to settle things momentarily. And then, he couldn't not go, what would they think of him? Perhaps someone would come to look for him, thinking that he was ill. That was all he needed!

He went, therefore.

He found the household in the midst of preparations for the wedding. Etiolated dressmakers were sewing chemises and shirts by hand, drowned in percale almost as pale as them

A tall, stiff woman, bent double next to a table, was tailoring full cloth. The long scissors chewed with a dull purr, and when she tore a strip with a single stroke it was like a whistling wind, an ascending scale that she cut abruptly when she arrived at the edge.

Julienne was crocheting, awkwardly, between her fiancé and her mother when the woman with the scissors said: "Madame, I've finished the three dozen and I still have a length of cloth; is it necessary to commence something else?"

"No, leave it; it might come in handy later," replied Madame Bujat, airily. "Perhaps for a layette," she added, seeing that no one had understood and not wanting her insinuation to go to waste.

Suddenly, Julienne dropped her crochet hook and fled, blushing.

"Let's leave the women to their stupidities," said Uncle Bujat, addressing Félix, "and let's go smoke a cigar in my room; we need to talk."

When the door was closed he exhibited his account books, in which the prosperity of the pharmacy appeared evidently, as radiant as a sun. He specified the conditions: Julienne would have eighty thousand francs and the pharmacy.

He intended to do things well. He knew, moreover that his future son-in-law was an intelligent and capable man, and that with him, the pharmacy and Julienne would be in good hands.

The banns were published, and the day of the wedding fixed for two weeks hence.

On returning home, Félix Guimau was a different man. The necessity of making a decision imposed itself to such an extent that everything became simple, being inevitable.

Behind the house there was a small garden where Norette amused herself cultivating salad vegetables, radishes and flowers. The walls of the neighboring properties enclosed that little terrain, in the middle of which, taking up most of the space, a superb circle of red geraniums was as flamboyant as a bouquet fallen into a well.

With Norette's small spade, Félix took up the geraniums carefully, in order not to damage the roots. It was a crepuscular starry night, which permitted him to act with precision.

When he had finished, he dug.

In spite of the poor equipment, his work was finished with the first light of dawn—but the hardest part still remained to do.

Without giving himself time to reflect, he climbed up to the first floor and came back down again, carrying the body of his mistress on his back, which he threw into the deep hole. Then, methodically, in an orderly manner, he set about covering it.

Soon, the soil was leveled and he replanted the geraniums, in a circle, as before. The sky was beginning to resemble opaque muslin extended over a pale flame.

Then he looked at the flowery tomb tenderly.

He sensed that it was all finished: the anguish and the nightmares, and the absurd emotions.

Also finished were all the joys that she had given him.

He was now going to furnish his career.

✳

A fortnight later, he married his cousin. At the champagne, after the wedding dinner, which was truly perfect, as Félix, on a memory of Norette that had returned brutally, was unable to repress an idiotic tear, Uncle Bujat leaned confidentially toward his ear.

"What! Black butterflies? We know what that's like; we've all passed through it. Flirtations, escapades . . . well, it's necessary that youth passes. But it's over; you've buried your bachelor life."

A SCANDAL

To Alphonse Allais.[1]

I

MISS THOMPSON, one of the best seamstresses of Flipp & Co. of New York, spent her Sunday in her habitual fashion.

Having got up at seven o'clock for breakfast, she went back up to her room, the door of which she locked with a double turn.

Then, after having taken a large bottle of rye whisky from the linen cupboard, Miss Thompson started to empty it slowly but surely, slumped in a rocking chair.

The little glass passed with an automatic regularity from the insipid tone of crystal with nothing in it to the rejoicing red-gold tone borrowed from the English alcohol—which, as everyone knows, has the strength of several horses.

---

1 Alphonse Allais (1854-1905) was a journalist best known as a humorist, who was one of the stars of the Chat Noir's improvised cabaret, often performing as half of a double act with Charles Cros or George Auriol.

As for the young and not unpleasant face of Miss Thompson, it retained an unalterable serenity; only a delicate carmine—which resembled the carmine of modesty like two drops of water—rose like a dawn under the warming influence (I am told) of the "enchanting liquor."

✳

On the wall, Miss Thompson saw, with an increasing exaltation, framed prints representing scenes from the Bible: *Agar in the Desert*; *Magdalen at the feet of Christ*— with hair so long that one might have thought it an advertisement for some capillary lotion. Alongside was *Washington's General Staff*: the great American on a prancing horse beside Lafayette, as if in a circus. The mounts, with an astonishing resemblance to wooden horses, were trampling with their hooves the dirty sugar that represented snow, where the fir trees in the foreground were so small, in comparison with the illustrious cavaliers, that one might rather have thought them a salad garnished with delusions of grandeur.

But Miss Thompson's eye, increasingly drowned by ecstasy, returned to the Biblical prints, and her bosom heaved, stirred by a sacred disturbance, while her hand, having become tremulous, leafed through the hymn-book on the table.

She sighed again, her eyes attached to the well-combed beard of the Lord: "Oh, Dear! Dear!" Then she got up, without too much difficulty, and went to sit down at the harmonium, which soon spread suave religious melodies under her hands.

On the floor below, Mr. Lowendal and Mrs. Brown, who were beginning to become drowsy in one another's arms—it is not good for one to go back to bed immediately after breakfast—awoke again delectably.

"Isn't it nice! Isn't it nice!" murmured the wife of the policeman Brown—who was on duty that Sunday in the distant district of Brooklyn—into the neck of her lover.

The canticles slowly wept by the harmonium, made the amorous couple dream of an ascent to Paradise—a comfortable ascent, without any haste to arrive, sustained by little negro angels, for preference, because that race has no fear of heavy tasks and Mrs. Brown was beginning to weigh her eighty kilos.

That did not prevent her from being an exquisite and very enthusiastic mistress for Mr. Lowendal—only her husband found her virtue a trifle glacially austere.

The penetrating music even softened the mores of the enlaced couple to such an extent that further kisses, mute but well-informed, caused them to faint into a decisive embrace.

Up above, the harmonium fell silent. Doubtless Miss Thompson was abandoning herself to a silent and edifying ecstasy, or perhaps she had simply fallen asleep—the sleep of the just, which resembles in such a striking fashion the sleep of the drunk.

The eyelids of the two lovers were fluttering again with tender lassitude when, from the room opposite, the sounds of a piano reached them.

This time, they were brought upright by an abrupt movement, and sat stiffly, side by side, their eyes widened by fearful astonishment.

"Is it possible?" they declared, in unison, their hands joined, as if to ward off divine wrath with a prayer and deflect the thunderbolt ready to fall on the house where such a sacrilege was being perpetrated.

It was from the apartment of the French couple who had arrived the evening before that those criminal sounds were coming.

A waltz by Hervé.

A waltz!

Profane music on a Sunday!

"Oh, people are not wrong to say that the continent is lost in impiety and vice!" opined Mrs. Brown.

"The end of the Old World is nigh," added Mr. Lowendal, with conviction.

With that, they went to sleep, for they were very tired.

II

At two o'clock precisely, all the tenants gathered around the table in the dining room for lunch. A pretty young woman of eighteen, blonde and as delicately pink as a virgin dreamed by a pre-Raphaelite, served the food.

The meal was expedited with a vertiginous rapidity, as if between two trains, and in a silence only interrupted by a few sharp *don'ts* from the servant when one of the diners pinched her bottom, without the slightest laugh.

The cups of tea filled the atmosphere with a fine odorous mist, and a few words were exchanged.

"Mr. Brown isn't here today?" Mr. Lowendal asked his mistress over the table.

"No, he's on duty," replied the spouse of the fortunate policeman.

"You played us some beautiful music, Miss Thompson."

A taciturn but intense reprobation enveloped the French couple—a painter and his wife—because of the other music, which was an emanation of Hell.

An immeasurably tall gentleman, stiff and pale—who, when standing up, looked like a hanged man—noted the arrest of a restaurateur who served beer and wine on Sunday

The French gentleman, who was listening to the conversations with the concentration of which one gives proof when one does not understand a treacherous syllable of a language, must doubtless have seized a word in passing that gave him an idea, for, after having asked his wife for the key to his room he disappeared, and then came back with a bottle of old imported cognac.

The objective was not in doubt; it was evidently to drink after his coffee, perhaps offering some to his wife.

And in front of everyone!

On a Sunday!

That rendered the boarders stupid with indignation, who now deserted the dining room sighing, overwhelmed

"Isn't it an abomination?"

"Shocking!"

And Miss Thompson, going up to her room briskly in order to shut herself away, darted at Mrs. Brown, who was also going back: "And yet, it's so easy to be correct."

THE LAMP

To M. Marcel Schwob.[1]

THAT day, Gaston Lagnier came out of Mademoiselle Gabrielle's apartment perfectly dazed by joy. However, he had found her again, and had even left her (O vain and fastidious Erinnyes) with that simpleton Fongerelle, who had become for a week the hateful shadow of the charming and delicate young woman with whom Gaston was madly in love.

But as he was about to depart, horribly unhappy, with the nausea of jealousy and a formidable desire to demolish something—including young Fongerelle—the beloved stood up, as the rising dawn dissipates bad dreams, and cooed, almost over the heart of her tortured lover: "Come and pick me up this evening; we'll go to Monsieur M***'s to laugh at the follies in verse of our friends the great men." And putting into her voice an ineffable hush: "I'll be alone."

---

1 The journalist Marcel Schwob (1867-1905) made a name for himself with Poesque short stories, many of them published in the *Écho de Paris*, of which he was the literary editor for a time.

Gaston Lagnier, the delicate and proud artist, had arrived at being content with those rogations of favors.

In the street, when he had emerged, the mud of the sidewalks had for him the soft caress of a Smyrna carpet. All the injuries, all the rancors—even the jealousy—were forgotten: everything, apart from the soft and somber gleam of her eyes, like two eternal flames in mysterious sanctuaries.

At eight o'clock precisely, he was transported to the beauty's lodgings. He did not intend as yet to find her. He would wait, walking back and forth under her windows, as in romances. It would be charming.

She was there, though. The window of the bedroom was illuminated and he could see the globe of the lamp designed on the curtain. He started to climb the stairs slowly, savoring the steps, like good things of which nothing more would soon remain; he would have liked her to live on the thirty-sixth, but he was outside her door.

That devil of a door had something intimidating about it, and he never rang immediately. He remained there for a moment, his heart in revolution, almost with a desire to go away, and then rang the doorbell loudly.

This time, he leaned on the doorbell moderately.

She had probably not heard, for it was necessary for him to ring a second time.

No response.

Then, seized by vertigo, his ears full of a buzz of anguish, he continued to ring, without knowing exactly what he was doing, in order to hear the sound of the crazed bell.

Then, with a sudden consciousness of the ridicule there was in ringing thus at a door that did not want to open, he ran away.

✳

Certainly she was at home. Impossible to doubt it. Now he saw again the window of the bedroom, and on the curtain, the globe of the lamp was designed clearly.

Oh, the infernal coquetry. She wanted to know, then, that he was there, dying of jealous rage, while she must be in the arms of the odious Fongerelle.

Yes, she was with him; doubtless they had not even quit one another.

And Gaston Lagnier departed, so wounded, so bleeding, that his amour was stunned, left for dead.

But the lighted window fascinated him; it seemed to radiate happiness. And he was subject to the attraction of evil things, of dolorous and cruel things.

He ended up going to sit down on the terrace of a café from which he could still see the monstrous and irresistible window.

No shadow appeared on the curtain—and that seemed to him to be the most horrible thing of all. He remembered the big bed with the batistes, all perfumed with her!

All his dearest memories rose up against him to make his sadness more heart-rending.

One day, at Trouville, she had had the whim of being taken for a trip at sea. He saw her again coming toward him barefoot in the fine sand, which was gray and as soft as a fur. The moist sunlight, the pale coppery sunlight of beaches, clung on to specks of gold in her Florentine bronze hair . . .

She came slowly, triumphantly, designed with precision by her bathing costume, and he followed with a kneeling gaze the elegant line by which her legs climbed to her hips, like a superb funereal urn.

It was a truly hideous crime that was being accomplished behind that window.

And still no shadow appeared on the curtain. He would have liked to see one, even if she were with the other . . . especially if she were with the other . . .

The window, radiant and tranquil, was blinding him and killing him.

At present, another memory leapt at his throat, desolating all his nerves and soaking them like a warm bath of tears, diluting even his wrath.

It was the memory of a walk in a forest, last summer.

The branches enlaced one another like a cathedral vault, where invisible footsteps scarcely rustled among the svelte birches clad in white robes like choirboys. Under the light passing through the foliage as if through a stained-glass window they recited verses exalted by kisses. But as a breeze swayed the sizzling censers of the ferns in the air, they bent their knees, overwhelmed by fervor—and she gave herself thus for the first time to his long desire, an absolute offering of all her ecstatic being.

O infinite misery! It was to the other that she was giving herself thus, there, close at hand. And he evoked the probable scene with a crucifying complaisance. He reviewed the familiar details in which, with the same abandon, the savant grace was never forgotten: the brown curls composed over the ear and the pretty fold of the bare arm that blossomed like a lotus in the lace, framing marvelously, with her fresh pallor, the languid torches of her eyes.

An immense dolor rolled its ever-recommencing waves within him, like an ocean. Then the anger returned, an anger exasperated by the imperious, despotic desire for *her*, for *her*, quivering with her treason, and he got up in order to run to the accursed door, sensing the force to smash it into smithereens with a single blow of his fist.

Abruptly, he calmed down, seeing that there were people looking at him. And an atonal meditation devoid of thought riveted his eyes to the luminous window, which now seemed to be a diabolical cascade of light devoid of any precise significance . . .

✳

He finally tore himself away from that torturing obsession and fled like a hunted man, marching at random.

The wet sidewalks had the dull sheen of dormant water into which the street-lamps allowed long streaks of fire to filter, and the lanterns of fiacres danced weakly in the mist.

In the sky, no stars; only the moon appeared, veiled by fog, veiled like a widow, paled by ancient chagrins.

The passers-by visibly had on their faces a cruel snigger for his humiliating dolor, and the mocking whistles of street-urchins were doubtless intended for him. So he applied himself to having an appearance "like everyone else," with an effort so assiduous that he forgot his distress therein.

He arrived home, entirely mechanically. Immediately, he was handed a note. He recognized Mademoiselle Gabrielle's handwriting and, under the scrutinizing gaze of the concierge, he read with a detached air:

> *Don't curse me my dear friend, curse my dressmaker; she has sent me my heliotrope dress—the one for which I've been waiting for a fortnight—infamy! The corsage has a three centimeter gap. What means is there of not running to her right away? I can't wait for you, therefore, but I shall spend the evening at M***'s. Come to collect me there.*

The traitress is mocking me again, Lagnier said to himself; *I certainly shan't go.*

And he went, of course, immediately.

Mademoiselle Gabrielle was there, with a heliotrope dress that suited her delightfully.

As they left she took Lagnier's arm and, leaning on it very tenderly, said: "I owe you apologies; come and receive them at home."

Lagnier had a simultaneous desire to strangle her, to burst into sobs and to kiss her madly; he did nothing at all.

As they went into the bedroom Gabrielle exclaimed, with a pretty laugh: "Good! I forgot to extinguish my lamp when I went out; I never do otherwise."

Mademoiselle Gabrielle never knew why, when she had unfastened her heliotrope dress, brought to the degree of desired perfection by an expert retouch, Gaston took her in his arms so savagely and kissed her shoulders—which were very beautiful—while weeping.

THE *GÂTEAU DES ROIS*

To Georges Rodenbach.[1]

CHARLES has got up this morning in a vile mood. He had gone to bed saying to himself: *Family celebrations, what a bore!* It was at great expense of bad reasons that he had been able to escape dinner with his professor, but to give the slip to his mother's guests was more difficult, and he had ended up resigning himself to it.

Now he is having breakfast in front of a coke fire, which resembles a florescence of ferocious roses, between Mathilde and Jenne, his sisters, more charming today, having been permitted the innocent coquetry of a sprig of violets at the corsage. It is only during vacations from his course that Charles can have breakfast with the family. So they devote themselves to a thousand petty attentions that he accepts with a rather poor grace, fundamentally

---

1 The poet Georges Rodenbach (1855-1898) published his famous novella *Bruges-la-Mort* (1892) in the same year as the present collection. He supported Krysinska in her spat with Gustave Kahn in an article in the *Revue Bleue* in 1891.

irritated to be treated as a big baby. He ends up retiring under the pretext of a keen desire to work but, in reality, to search in his imagination for some good dodge that will render his evening free.

He does not find any, and returns to the dining room like a defeated wrestler.

The table was already laid, and on the dresser a "*gâteau des rois*" was displayed, solemn and mocking.[1] Mathilde and Jeanne, already dressed for dinner in pink cashmere dresses, were truly charming with their soft chestnut tresses, rolled up above the nape like beautiful slumbering serpents. His mother, who had gone to a great deal of trouble to supervise the preparations, had prettily colored cheeks, giving her a precious artificial youth beneath the white muslin of her hair.

He heard five o'clock chiming at the Sorbonne, and a luminous idea came to him: his professor's invitation. It was quite simple; the truth would come out later, but for this evening, he would be free.

It succeeded perfectly, and he slipped away "like a stag launched by a sure hand," as that great joker Maurice said, who was always telling such funny stories about brasseries of women. A lucky fellow, that one, who lived alone in a furnished room.

---

1 *Gâteau des rois* is the French name of the toroidal Occitan pastry also known as a tortell, traditionally eaten on Twelfth Night, with the idiosyncrasy described later in the story.

Charles arrived outside the brasserie of the Chien Savant. He had gone in there once before, with Maurice, who made him marvel with his fine jokes; for instance, he asked someone for a cigarette and put the whole packet in his pocket. He was as witty as possible.

He decided to go in, and collapsed on a banquette. The Chien Savant was empty, and the colored glass windows only allowed through a sad and grave light, that of a church or a sick-room. A cashier clad in black, evidently very distinguished, embarrassed him momentarily with her judgmental gaze, and then stretched out a pale hand, like a pianist leaning on a key.

That caused a fat woman of a certain age to surge forth with a bunch of flowers on her bosom and a nurse's apron, who asked him what he would have. He confessed that he desired a bitter Picon.

She brought a long glass on a zinc tray and poured the bitter Picon, and then filled a small glass with something dark.

"Me, I'll have a quinquina," she said, amiably, as she sat down next to Charles.[1]

He saw immediately that she was a good person, and, becoming bolder, asked her if she knew Maurice.

"A short stout fellow?"

"No, tall and thin."

"Exactly." She knew him very well, and even remembered having seen Charles with him.

"Your name is Louis?"

"No, Charles."

---

1 Like the orange-flavored Picon, the chinchona-bark flavored quinquina was a very popular aperitif in France in the 1890s.

"That's what I meant."

And immediately, she started addressing him familiarly.

"Are you offering me another quinquina?"

Without waiting for his reply, she ordered a quinquina in an administrative voice.

"You ought to have a quinquina too; it's very good for the stomach."

As he refused, fearing mixtures, she shouted: "And a qinquina—that makes two!"

Two more women had come to sit down, and also drank quinquinas. One was a dwarf who gave the impression of having had her legs amputated, with the head of a housewife. Her name was Bébé. The other, a blonde with the face of a saint of religious imagery had the padded roundness of an armchair. They all sang together:

> *Brown child of Venice*
> *With the mocking smile,*
> *I have to tell you*
> *The secret of my heart.*

Charles noticed that they did not have a great deal of conversation, but he found them very cheerful. His eyes having adapted to the obscurity he was able to distinguish in the depths of the room several tables united by extensions, which thus formed a long refectory table covered by a cloth.

"You'll stay and have dinner with us, Charlot," said the fat lady, moistening his cheek with a kiss, which intimidated him greatly.

He stammered a refusal.

"Yes, yes, you'll stay with your Niniche."

The gas was lit and the dubious Medievalism of the brasserie appeared, further dishonored by a few advertisements hung on the wall in fames: *Bal Bullier. Moutarde Bornibus. Choucroûte.*

The cashier quit her till and glided toward the back of the room after having said in a clear and reasonable voice: "Mesdames, to table."

As the bitter Picon had given him an appetite, he decided to stay, and he was sat down opposite the cashier, between Niniche and the woman with the face of a saint, whose name was Loulon. Plates were now circulated, which the cashier filled with soup, majestically.

The mixture of aperitifs did not succeed for him, for he found in the soup a very pronounced taste of grease; afterwards, beef was brought; that had no luck, he had a horror of beef—and then, all those quinquinas had made him feel sick.

The women fed themselves in great silence and Charles was gallantly pouring the wine when the waiter—a handsome fellow—put a plate of macaroni on the table. They insisted that he be served first; the macaroni was, moreover, detestable. It was overcooked, which gave it a striking resemblance to pasta glue, and reeked like an old dishcloth. They were absolutely insistent that he have some more, but he thanked them and refused energetically

The cashier was maternal. "Just a little more."

No, he was no longer hungry, word of honor.

In reality, he was dying of hunger and counted on catching up on the salad—but there wasn't any.

Niniche now began a story. The concierge had played a dirty trick on her of which she would never have thought him capable. Her strong person was very disturbed by it. Charles didn't understand very well; it was a matter of the *Petit Journal* and a chicken thigh. She concluded by saying that it was necessary not to have a heart in the life of this world, but that she would always be the same: sentiment would doom her. "Shall I tell you? I'm too stupid."

Bébé, personally, no longer had any illusions. Knowing full well that it was necessary to be "philosophical" nowadays; as for men she cared as little for them as the year forty.

The dessert was brought, consisting of plums and unbreakable gruyere. Charles was thinking about the exquisite things he could have been eating at home when a *gâteau des rois* was placed on the table.

That was too much!

The gâteau was circulated, covered with a napkin, and the ladies served it, handling it at length. He had to take the last piece that remained, and right away, nearly broke a tooth on the faience baby that was playing the fatal bean.

Then there were exclamations and laughter that disconcerted him completely. The cashier popped the cork of a bottle of champagne, which happened to be there, and everyone set about drinking and clinking glasses noisily to the health of the king.

Charles now thought with melancholy about the fifty-franc bill—his uncle's Christmas present—which was evidently about to pass.

It was necessary to choose a queen, and that embarrassed him greatly; he ended up deciding on the cashier, out of respect, and took a kiss from the side of her chin, which had the scent of tincture of iodine.

It was patriarchal.

He had the joy of seeing the table cleared and cups placed for the coffee. The quinquinas, the champagne and all the emotion had given him the commencement of a headache. Unfortunately, the coffee was fetid and even the cashier admitted that it was not as good as usual.

Niniche now moistened his cheeks again in a fit of tenderness, while suggesting a general round of finos

The brasserie became animated. An aged decorated monsieur took a tea sitting beside the saint, whispering into her neck his eyes ablaze, Bébé served beers to a dozen young men who had arrived in a band singing: "Holy Spirit, descend on us!" to the accompaniment of saucers banged on the table.

Niniche also had to quit him in order to go serve a young man who was very well-dressed and so pale that he seemed to have passed through Javel water,[1] with the consequence that Charles remained alone before the intact round of finos, with an increasing headache. Ashamed of not having been more amused, he suddenly imagined emptying all the glasses of fino in order to play a good joke on those ladies.

The saint, near the beer pump, was arguing with the waiter, who ended up giving her a slap. She went into

---

1 A solution of sodium or potassium hypochlorite, used as a household bleach.

a corner, sobbing, and then abruptly slid to the floor. She was now seen twitching between Niniche and Bébé, who emptied carafes over her face and unfastened her. Charles was able to perceive the fringe of a red corset, which filled him with compassion for the person with such virginal eyes—but the finos were upsetting his stomach horribly.

Now the gas began to go out, and the cashier, ringing her bell precipitately, sent the waiter to fetch the gas-man.

In the dying light the brasserie was lugubrious. The rosewood counter resembled a sarcophagus, from which the black-clad cashier surged forth spectrally. Charles's headache had become unbearable, and his nausea augmented to the point that he had to absent himself for a few minutes and came back with a distraught face. He called Niniche in order to settle up as quickly as possible; his bill came to forty-seven francs eighty; it was complete ruin.

As Niniche returned his change, very lazily, waiting for him to tell her to keep it, a battle started in the brasserie. It was the brayhards from Bébé's tables who were falling in a mob on the young man passed through Javel water. Yielding to a chivalrous impulse, Charles tried to intervene, and immediately received a punch that made his nose bleed.

Policemen arrived and, understanding nothing of what had happened, wanted to take Charles to the station. Fortunately, he managed to escape, went home abominably ill, and went to bed immediately.

His astonishment was great on seeing that the clock only marked ten o'clock. The evening had seemed so long!

Now, the freshness of the sheets calmed him and cured him.

Meanwhile, from the drawing room where people were still lingering, taking tea, a faint sound of mingled voices arrived, chatting in the midst of the tender quietude of soft armchairs in the pleasant warmth of a coke fire, like a florescence of ferocious roses.

THE MIDNIGHT EXAMINATION

To M. Catulle Mendès.[1]

WHEN young Baronne Lucienne de Charmantré found herself alone after the departure of her friend—who doesn't have friends, alas?—there was, in that elegant drawing room, in the corner of the little mauve sofa embroidered with maize, an explosion of despair as in the climax of a tragedy by Aeschylus.

Deceived! She was deceived by her husband, scarcely a year after the solemn and joyful wedding day.

She would have preferred to be forever unaware of that hideous circumstance, and rancor awoke in her against the pitiless "friend" who had just informed her of it.

And with that cynical old Italian, that Contessa Pittani, with the black hair, varnished like the panels of a brand new carriage!

---

1 Catulle Mendès (1841-1909) was the most prolific supplier of short fiction to *fin-de-siècle* newspapers and his risqué vignettes of contemporary Parisian life, especially, were very distinctive; the present story is a pastiche thereof. He was the literary editor of the *Écho de Paris* for a while, and supported Krysinska's claim to be the pioneer of *vers libre*.

Going to stand before a mirror that reflected her gracious age calmed the young baronne's great chagrin slightly.

Under the illumination of the pink candles burning in the brackets, the light waves of her delicate red hair seemed the very tresses of the dawn; and that matutinal evocation was continued in the pale freshness of her complexion, in the gleam of the bright, slightly green-tinted eyes, which resembled two lively springs reflecting branches, and in the flavorsome fruit of the mouth, in which the little milky nuts of the teeth glinted softly.

But she fell back, numbed by pain, into the hollow of the elegant sofa—mauve embroidered with maize—mortally distressed by that affront to her beauty.

"What, then, can she have that's better than me? Oh, I'd be very curious to know, certainly . . ."

Dreaming thus, very sadly, Lucienne passed into the bedroom, for midnight was chiming the derisory hour of repose. She sent Victorine away, who came to undress her, and, having locked her door with a double turn she stood bolt upright before the large looking-glass, in the calm light of the illuminated lamps.

With an impatient hand, she struggled with the entanglement of clasps, caught in the folds of the peignoir—a lovely peignoir in heavy blue Byzantine silk with a decoration of silver pearls—and the neck soon appeared, delicate and forceful.

Then the peignoir opened in a joyous yawn of the mauve surah that lined it and slid away with a tender whisper of fabric. Her arms, as proud as regal lilies, were radiant, and the shoulders with ingenuous dimples, il-luminated by blonde gleams, spread out amid the warm foam of the chemise, which resembled the snowy bubbles of a terribly heady wine on the rim of the frail cup of the corset.

Then, the bite of the whalebone let go in its turn; the petticoats were shed one by one and fell like a set of perfumed petals.

The chemise flew away like a mad butterfly, intoxicated by the aromas of the charming body, which then appeared in all the glory of its radiant youth.

And there was, in the intimacy of the socialite's bedroom, the unexpected evocation of underwood mythologies, and the encounter before that dazzled mirror of some bewildered nymph.

From the rosy conquering heel all the way to the delicate curls, also rosy, which fluttered above the eyes, the entire line was harmonious and pure, voluptuously flowered by two perfect breasts. The shadows nestling in the most tender retreats were transparent and gilded, while the light kissed the firm elegance of the reliefs softly.

In order not to be satisfied by that examination, it would have required the young baronne to be entirely deprived of esthetic sense, and even of common sense.

Thus, a consoled smile illuminated her gracious lips, which ceased pouting.

But not for long.

Because, in that pretty little argumentative head, an objection had surged forth: A woman cannot judge a woman's beauty, according to men.

What was she to do, then?

She could not, however, address herself to a male expert without falling into the lamentable repetition of reprisals that one undertakes to avenge oneself on a lover without being drawn by amour.

Suddenly, she had an idea—a luminous one, I promise you.

At the last Salon, on the day of the private view, she had remained petrified by admiration before a "Drunken Bacchante," to such an extent that she had not noticed an enraged trampler who had torn the demi-train of her bottle-green bengaline dress embroidered with Japanese gold, which was a marvel.

The artist who had translated the living and vibrant flexibility of that torso must be a connoisseur of feminine beauty.

His name—Jean Chastenay—remained engraved in her memory. Tomorrow, no later, she would look for his address in the Salon catalogue.

The next day, in fact, at the hour of excursions in the Bois, Lucienne de Charmantré simply climbed into a fiacre and had herself taken to the painter' studio.

Her idea was very simple; it was a matter of nothing less than offering herself as a model.

If, after the proof, the famous artist accepted her, it was because she did not merit the insult that the baron had inflicted on her, and, thus armed with self-confidence, she would be well able to reconquer him.

The fiacre stopped in the Boulevard de Clichy, and the young baronne set out to climb the copious staircase leading to the studio. An apprehension gripped her now, and a little emotion too, perfectly legitimate. The painter must evidently be very old.

"Evidently," because she desired him to be.

But her error did not last any longer than the chime of the doorbell—which she agitated furiously. Jean Chastenay, a sturdy and handsome fellow about thirty years old, opened the door himself and enquired about the purpose of the visit with a distracted simplicity.

". . . Model," stammered Lucienne.

"Ah! Very good, my child, we'll see about that; go and undress behind the screen."

The baronne took refuge, half-dead of emotion, in the retreat indicated, regretting the folly of her expedition.

Run away? It was necessary not to think of it. And then, an invincible curiosity was stirring her at the same time.

When Lucienne reappeared, draped uniquely in a flower-patterned dust-coat, the painter, who had resumed work, uttered an indolent "Let's go" that sounded clearly the fall of the last veils.

In the frank daylight that came from the large window she appeared then, clad only in the slender pin of blonde tortoiseshell planted in her hair.

"Superb! Superb!" exclaimed Jean Chastenay, stunned by admiration. "But you're miraculously beautiful, my child, quite simply, and I'll hire you on whatever conditions you wish."

The proof had succeeded, and Lucienne, triumphant and dying of shame, fled behind the screen, where Jean Chastenay followed her, fascinated, losing his head.

So radiant was the glorious nudity of the young woman—only defended by the almost sacred grace of beauty, that the painter remained annihilated by adoration, in a quasi-religious ecstasy.

But as Lucienne, half-dressed, reassembled with quivering hands her scattered garments, she found herself abruptly in the arms of the young man, who embraced her recklessly, brutally . . . with kisses of an imploring ardor on her divine neck, her eyes, her mouth . . . in which they stifled the distress ready to scream like a hind with its throat cut . . . and Lucienne collapsed amid the rugs, wildly conquered—and then, O miracle, abandoned herself with a profound sob, thunderstruck by a suddenly-revealed joy, of which her husband had never even enabled her to divine the first syllable.

Having returned home, the young baronne did not take long to observe the excellent results of the regime that she had imagined.

The baron perceived for the first time that his wife was delectable, doubtless because of the marvelous assurance that Lucienne had acquired, and perhaps because of the mysterious radiation that embellishes the faces of women who have palpitated, if only for the interval of one forgettable minute, in the reckless hands of amour.

But the new assiduities of the husband who had become, too late, his wife's lover, now seemed rather importunate to Lucienne.

A short time later, the baron, having encountered Jean Chastenay by chance at his club, felt sympathetically attracted to him, with a remarkable surety of instinct. The young painter frequented the Hôtel de Chrmantré enormously, and painted a marvelous portrait of the baronne, which won the medal of honor at the Salon.

SNOWY TALES

THE MIRROR
A Christmas Story

To Georges Darien.[1]

BOGUNIA is definitely already a big girl.

Last Christmas Eve, after the solemn meager supper at which everyone sat down as soon as the first star appeared in the sky, something inadmissible had happened when they went into the room where the Christmas tree had been prepared in great mystery, iluminated by little yellow, blue, pink and green candles, the perfume of which had mingled delectably with the odor of fir-wood.

Bogunia ran to the table, covered with a white cloth, where the toys were fulgurant, and took possession unceremoniously of a superb doll sitting in an armchair

---

1 Georges Darien (1862-1921) was an outspoken polemicist whose angry works of fiction, including a quasi-autobiographical account of life in a military prison camp, obtained a certain *succès de scandale.*

like a natural person. There was mad general laughter, and a great shame for her, because the doll was for her young sister Wladia. She had the unpardonable weakness to weep, in spite of the surprise of a de luxe edition of a Mickiewicz, with her initials in gold.

Then her fifteen years were thrown at her head.

She had retained a bad memory of that evening, and did not like anyone to talk about it, which was precisely what that little horror Wladia never failed to do.

That year brought a multitude of changes for Bogunia; her dresses became long, and the peasants who came to the *dwor*, instead of simply bowing to the ground, as they had before, now touched the hem of her garment with their bonnets: the fashion in which masters are saluted in Slav countries.

All of that resembles a conspiracy of sorts.

And the mirror is mixed up in it; it attracts her at present, as the water of the pond once had, in which she watched the clouds pass in the other sky down below, the singular sky where plants also grew and which seemed to be a sky apart, known only to her.

The vertical and moving waters of the pivoted looking-glass have something of that mystery. The room and the furniture reflected therein, although familiar, are not exactly the same, but rather their dreamed resemblance.

Younger, she was enraged by not being able to go in there. Now she sees a beautiful young woman that she does not yet know very well: tall, with an elegant corsage, as in portraits, and a slightly pale flowery complexion in which the eyes, larger, are astonished.

Christmas is approaching again, a Christmas with no hope of a doll—but she mocks dolls now.

She has devoured the poetry of Mickiewicz, and many other books. She has a hunger for reading, which is not yet an occupation of the mind for her, but only a captivating game in which it is a matter of divining enigmas. All the scenes of passion, all the amorous conflicts, are the growling of the sphinx, and the words are not so much words as a special and suggestive music, carrying dreams, as the sea does shellfish.

What charms her most of all are the tales of old Walkowa on the evenings when the peasant women, with somnambulistic gestures, wind the hemp, the mordant odor of which floats under the beams of the ceiling, from which bunches of rosemary hang down.

While her box-wood fingers manipulate stout knitting needles, here is the story of the *Stchyga*, which, as everyone knows, is the ghost of a newborn arrived in the world with all its teeth; such children only live for a few days, and generally die unbaptized. Then, in the form of an owl, they haunt ruins and deserted places, making a vague wailing herd. Sometimes they keep their natural form, with an owl's wings.

A hundred years ago, a poor woman who was up late looking for a stray cow was returning to her *hata* at midnight, and behold—when she approaches a house destroyed by fire the previous winter, only the chimney of which remains standing, she hears a plaint coming from above, like that of a child, so sad that she stops dead, for the voice reminds her so much of the voice of her poor little Janko, who died a few weeks ago, unbaptized.

More dead than alive herself, she raises her eyes, and as the moon is full, she sees, perched on top of the ruin, her little Janko, in his natural skin, his chemise brighter than the snow, and an owl's wings on his shoulders.

He was weeping piteously, showing the double array of his little white teeth, like drops of milk: his teeth of a stchyga.

She remained there all night, without being afraid any longer, weeping and summoning him to her arms, but he was doubtless unable to come down, and he disappeared at cock-crow. The poor mother, heart-broken, had the coffin exhumed. It was empty.

Then she went to confide all that to an old and wise *kuma*, who advised her to have a mass said for the soul of the dead child and to suspend from the cross at the crossroads the chemise in which he had died. That is what she did. Then, after three days, she had the coffin opened again.

This time, the little cadaver reposed there, in his chemise brighter than snow, strewn with the fallen feathers of the wings he had borne when he was a stchyga.

Then there was the fantastic story of Lataviec, a celestial spirit that descends to earth when people think they are seeing a shooting star. Those spirits are attracted by the charm of amour toward some beautiful village girl.

The strange lover appears to the one he has chosen in the form of a marvelous adolescent, with floating golden hair and wings on his back. But when he is recalled to Heaven by an order that he cannot disobey, the beauty, left alone with the memory of a superhuman felicity, soon dies of languor.

It is for that reason that beautiful young women are seen whose eglantine cheeks become akin to pale jasmine flowers, and whom an incurable melancholy brings back to the solitary and dear places where the ideal lover appeared, until they die.

The most impressive thing was to hear narrated the various means that young women have of knowing what husband is destined for them in future, especially this one:

On Christmas Eve the young woman must shut herself in a room alone, and, having lit candles in front of a mirror, await the stroke of midnight; then, in the mirror, the man that she is bound to marry will appear.

Oh, it was tempting to try that! But to shut oneself away alone at midnight . . . and then, was there not something diabolical about it? For Christmas Eve belongs to the holy delight caused by the birth of Jesus, and all the faithful are at midnight mass; it would therefore be necessary to invent some lie in order to avoid it. However, to know what the future husband will be like is attractive.

What if he were to resemble Monsieur Bronislaw, who danced with her last winter . . . and, I believe, palpitated a little too . . . it's not impossible that he might have those tender brown eyes . . .

Her decision is made; she will try.

It is not difficult to pretend to be ill. It will not even be entirely a lie, for emotion renders her weak in advance, at the mere idea of the proof.

✳

Bogunia has shut herself in the vast room into which no one ever comes, which was the reception hall in the days of the Jagiello kings, when national hospitality, the famous Slavic hospitality, was practiced in epic proportions. At great family feasts the lord invited all his living friends from several *versts* around to sit down at his table. Into the profound *puhary* the fermented honey ran, and on the dressers the huge pieces of venison fumed, while in the monumental fireplace, a joyous martyr, a fir-log with all its branches was consumed, the resinous aroma of which embalmed the hall.

The fireplace is black and empty now; and Bogunia does not really know whether the frisson that is making her shoulders undulate like a pretty movement of chilly wings comes from cold or fear.

In front of the tall mirror, slightly green-tinted and slightly tarnished, like a glaucous pool in which so many gracious faces came to sink, forgotten today even in verses—the last courtiers—Bogunia has placed the silver candlesticks in which odorous wax candles are burning.

She sees the colossal beam that supports the ceiling, made of an entire oak tree, the ridge of which, catching the light, is like a long, thin sword above her head.

The truth is that Bogunia is dying of fear and thinking seriously of fleeing.

At that moment, the first stroke of midnight sounds, which immobilizes her with fear.

The second stroke follows, and then the third. Bogunia begins to mock her credulity and to look at the mirror with slight suspicion through her lashes.

The fourth and fifth strokes.

She now has a grimace of disappointment; it would have been so pleasant, that fugitive glimpse of her husband, and she holds it against him for missing the rendezvous.

The sixth and seventh strokes.

Bogunia, with the cry of someone wounded, falls to the floor, unconscious.

In the mirror, very distinctly, Death has appeared to her.

The sinister prediction was nearly realized, and poor Bogunia came very close to "marrying Death," for the impression was terrible and she fell gravely ill in consequence; but her youth combated heroically, and triumphed.

A slight pallor in her refined features and delicate violets on her eyelids that make her eye prettier, that is all that remains of the bad quarter of an hour, which she is beginning to forget.

Monsieur Bronislaw presented himself at the new year's festivities, and she truly has no more need to inter-rogate anyone to know who her husband will be, since Monsieur Bronislaw loves her and has asked her father for her. Next autumn, she will be his wife.

Spring is approaching but the last snows are still dormant in the country, like the precious furs of the polar bear, careless of the warm sunlight that is sowing dazzling gems therein.

Oh, what a joy it would be to take advantage of the rides in a low-slung sleigh, which runs so vertiginously fast, while the bells of the harness tinkle monotonously and delightfully.

Bogunia wishes for it continually when she allows herself to be surprised by a little dream and distracted from the blissful prostration in the present felicity, next to him, in the midst of that nuptial landscape.

Then, spring brings new delights: the frissons of young foliage and the odorous snow of lilacs.

Then summer.

And the time goes quickly, as quickly as the low sleigh; and the enchanted tinkle of the little bells that will accompany their timid kisses will soon be lost in the sound of church bells, the triumphant and marvelous bells of marriage.

Now the great day has arrived, and the unforgettable moment is nigh.

The procession, in order to depart, is only waiting for her. Her sister Wladia and the demoiselles of honor go to make sure that everyone is ready, after casting a slightly jealous glance at the gracious vision of Bogunia, radiant in the whiteness of lace, under the imponderable waves of the veil, which the candlelight causes to stream like a silver dew.

Left alone, Bogunia follows with a dreamy gaze the familiar details of her virginal bedroom, which she is quitting with a joyful affection.

Her gaze goes to the mirror, which reflects her charming image, transfigured for the glorious offering of amour.

But an odious memory, the memory of that ominous Christmas night, makes her recoil, fearfully, with an abrupt movement. At that moment, one of the candles bites the light veil, and in an instant, the bride, enveloped in flame, is a tragic torch herself.

When people came running in response to the young woman's screams it was too late. Bogunia died in her bridal gown, and the sinister prediction was accomplished; Death came to keep its promise.

BARCIEÏ

To Monsieur Anatole France.[1]

Oh, that Barcieï, oh, that strange youth!

In love with his beautiful Ukrainian soil as with a beautiful young woman.

Caring, like a miser for his ducats, for his bees, donors of perfumed honey: the honey that he knows better than anyone how to age in skins to become the famous hydromel, with the color of the sun and the taste of flowers.

So, when Barcieï comes to survey the patient labor of the hives, the familiar bees never repel him with the

---

1 The great Anatole France (1844-1924) was the most prestigious of all Krysinska's supporters in the controversy regarding the pioneering of *vers libre*.

menace of their stings, but assemble in buzzing and joyful crowns above his head, as blond as their wings.

Blond he is, that young Slav peasant, grown up in the serene ambiance of an agrarian life. Blond like King Piast, the original lord of pagan Slavia.[1]

The mild ocean of the Steppes isolates this corner of the earth, as fertile as a paradise in which people have retained the soul of the first humans.

But Bariceï is much wilder than other boys of his age. The beautiful country girls with gilded tresses frighten him. He prefers, at harvest time, the caress on his hands of ripe crops—which are like the gilded tresses of the beautiful country girls.

He has never even understood, the simpleton, the faithful and tender love that there is in the eyes of Magdusia—in those eyes, which, by a special grace of the gods, are dark, although her hair is as pale as wild oats.

Only once was the wily girl able to draw him to dance at the *karczma*. But as Barcieï did not know how to dance, she took the first cavalier who came along, for she wanted at least to dance in front of him.

The fiddler, seated at the table, with the broad gesture of a sower, launched into the rhythm of the mazurka; and the boys stamped their heels, and then took hold of the women like prey, spinning them around madly. Then tresses floated like flags, under the crowns of foliage with which Ukrainian young women make diadems.

---

1 Piast the Wheelwright was the legendary but probably fictitious founder of the first dynasty of kings of Poland, which lasted from the tenth century to the fourteenth.

And coral necklaces also bounded over the ample white chemises embroidered with bright colors. And the short red-striped skirts were inflated with air like the sails of ships.

The admirable northern dance, heroic and tender at the same time, separated the couples momentarily. Then they ran across the vast izba, the left arm of the man around the waist of his partner, whom he was almost carrying, while his right hand held his astrakhan czapka high in the air, as if for a solemn oath. "Hei! Hei Hei ze ha!" sang the leading couple. And the violin wept with joy and laughed nervously, in bursts, like someone possessed, and then sobbed again, like a human throat, and palpitated like a heart oppressed by excessively tender memories and vain desires.

Now, Magdusia, entirely given to the intoxication of the dance, almost forgot the strange youth that she loved—God knows—with all her soul.

He remained seated for a long time on a stool, listening to that music, without really seeing the Ukranianian maidens whose hair was floating like flags.

But where is Barcieï now?

Magdusia no longer wants to dance; all her joy has gone with the strange youth.

Barcieï has gone into the forest.

It is the hour when dusk is falling, the witching hour, and the hour when the fir trees are like accursed warriors raising a gesture of menace toward the sky that they are darkening.

The livid, almost supernatural light weeping through the branches brushes the tree trunks like a flutter of anxious wings.

On the ground, the mushrooms draw together, for mysterious confidences, their heads turbaned with pale cloth.

In that consternated immobility and that formidable silence—the sound of footsteps awakens innumerable feet that flee, fearful and troubled, or perhaps approach.

And in the resinous perfumes—like torches burned at funerals—the miraculously tender mosses are like beds inviting to the long dreamless sleep, the tranquil sleep of death.

"Hei! Hei!" sings Magdusia's beloved, Barcieï, whose soul expands in that limpid and intoxicating air.

"Hei! Hei!" reply voices hidden among the fir trees.

Suddenly, Barcieï stops, as immobile as the trees themselves: immobilized by fear.

Is that not something white, asleep, lying there in the midst of the mosses?

No, it's only a movement of the bright soil, illuminated by that livid—almost supernatural—light weeping through the branches.

But this time it is an apparition . . . infernal or celestial?

Oh, doubtless celestial!

For her beauty is so fascinating that the chaste Barcieï hears his heart cry amour toward her, and he follows with a light step the nymph that is fleeing toward the darkness of the woods.

Her beautiful arms are bare; and her luminous breasts and hips with virginal lines are veiled by a tunic of foliage. But the miracle is her hair, as green as the foliage that veils the virginal lines of her loins.

Alas, on seeing that hair, Barcieï has understood; it is the Rusalka, goddess of the woods, marvelous and perfidious, who attracts young men into the depths of the forest, where they find an exquisite and certain death.

Is it necessary, then, to flee?

And Barcieï hesitates, palpitating with fear and delirious tenderness.

At that moment, the Rusalka also stops and turns her face toward him,

Her green eyes are shining like springs enlivened by sunlight.

And her curved mouth of a fauness, as red as the fruit of the sorb tree, is laughing silently.

❋

The next day, when Magdusia comes into the wood to pick mushrooms for her old father's dinner, she finds Barcieï dead at the foot of a fir tree.

Hei! Hei! It is in vain that the young men hail her for the dance. Magdusia wanders in taciturn places, a shadow in the dolor of loving—until the day when, her pain being too heavy, she will throw herself into the pale waters of the pond.

Then, as happens to all virgins who have drowned, she will be one of the undines that are seen on lunar nights circling together—but enlaced—near rushes. And in order to avenge her scorned amour, she will cause men to perish in the water, attracted to her by the melancholy charm of her voice . . . unless, before then, she encounters on a sunlit Sunday, when the ripe crops are like the gilded tresses of beautiful country girls, another youth with soft eyes.

For it might then be the case that she will follow him to the karczma, where, in the diabolical rhythm of the mazurka, one forgets old dolors.

"Hei! Hei! Hei ze ha!"

. . . And afterwards, to the church.

MANIA AND MARYSIA

To Charles Maurras.[1]

Both sixteen years old, and both having the melancholy and grave beauty of Ukrainian girls, with vast eyes as blue as nocturnal skies and heavy brown hair, Mania and Marysia resembled two sisters when, with their arms around one another's waists, they wandered solitarily in the dormant heaths and the livid clearings in the fir woods.

---

1 Charles Maurras (1868-1952) was at the opposite end of the political spectrum to many of the other dedicatees featured in the volume, but that was not yet obvious in 1892, and he supported Krysinska in the *vers libre* controversy. It is unlikely, however, that his ultra-Catholicism would have allowed him to approve of this story.

They were, however, only friends—but so perfectly loving!

Orphans, neither of them had known her father, overworked laborers who had died young. And in each of them the memory bled of a tragic day when men in black garments carried away her tender mother, her dear mafoula, her unique matoulenka, in order to lay her in the tomb.

Mania and Marysia have known one another since early childhood, but it was only when Mania, the latter to dress in mourning, bewildered and sobbing, had thrown her arms around Marysia's neck as they emerged from the church where the funereal candles were still burning, that their tenderness became powerful to the point of being reckless.

And it was not without charm, that isolation of two virginal hearts, in the midst of sturdy agrarian life and in the midst of that harsh, grim and maleficent landscape, where the marvelous lies in ambush under every osier grove, murmurs in every spring and gallops over the plains in the evening at a stealthy, furtive pace . . .

Mania and Marysia lived in the same hata and cultivated a small plot of land that sufficed for their almost unreal existence of little angels.

In the evening, while spinning, they intoxicated themselves with superstitious fear, with legendary tales in which their young memory was already rich.

Such as that of the man who, waking up at midnight once on the edge of a meadow where fatigue had over-

126

taken him, perceived a woman standing nearby. As he examined her curiously he realized that she had the feet of an animal. When, having returned to the village, he had recounted his vision, no one was astonished to see, shortly thereafter, mortality rife in the cowsheds, for the specter perceived had been none other than the Death of Cows.

The same personified presentiment enables Cholera to appear in the form of a woman wearing red boots and a coral necklace, walking on water and sighing sadly.

The specter of malaria is an old woman with hen's feet. One man who had seen her fell dangerously ill and was only cured by a remedy of which he had dreamed three times, which was mare's milk.

Then, treasures that are weary of lying dormant in the earth can offer themselves, reveal their presence by some supernatural sign: a blue flame, a cat, or a naked child running precipitately around the place where buried gold can be found.

Very pious, Mania and Marysia did not miss any solemnity of the church.

When, from their hata isolated on the road, they heard the holy bells appealing for the prayer, the two young solitaries ran in haste to carry to the feet of images shining with fine gold and bright colors the good offering of their little souls, as chaste as hollyhocks.

But when, after the office, the young men wanted to take them dancing, Mania and Marysia were frightened, like two wild grouse.

Thus, piously and virginally, they had promised one another always to live together without ever marrying.

Once, they were staying up late, spinning hemp by the light of the resinous branches that were being consumed in the hearth.

The night outside was bright with stars and fallen snow. At times, the squall lifted up clouds of gravel, which struck the windows like a swarm of unquiet moths seeking refuge.

As midnight approached, the sound of the church bells arrived, slightly confused, as if veiled . . .

The orphans looked at one another, surprised. They knew the festivals of the calendar by heart, and none fell on that day. And then, that hour of the night . . .

"Undoubtedly, we only thought we heard the bells."

But no. The bells were ringing. And their beautiful and sad voice floated languidly in the limpid air, like a boat on the water.

"Since the Lord is calling, it's necessary to obey. Let's go."

And the two friends, hastily covering their shivering shoulders with lambskins, set forth.

✳

The church, filled with the faithful, is dazzling, with all the candles lit.

The orphans sense their hearts freezing within them on seeing that motionless and mute crowd standing all around.

None of the familiar parishioners is there; nothing but strange faces of terrible aspect. They end up recognizing some, but they are people already dead.

The poor things try to pray fervently, without paying any heed to the sinister assembly.

Now the great door opened and the officiant appears before the master altar

When the old priest has turned toward the faithful, the young women are able to see his beard, hanging all the way to his waist and as white as milk, as is his hair, streaming over his shoulders. They recognize a pastor saint who died nearly a hundred years ago, whose portrait is hanging in the wall in the presbytery.

It is him, as he is seen in the painting, feature for feature, but with something tarnished in his jaundiced skin, as if by an immemorial mildew.

Mania perceived very close by her defunct godmother and, a little further away, her own dear mother. The latter remains indifferent, like a stranger, without even seeing her child, but the godmother leans toward the orphan and speaks hastily into her ear:

"What are you doing here, girl? For the love of God, flee! Flee quickly! And if you're pursued, throw everything you can behind you, or you're doomed!"

Hearing that, Marysia and Mania contrive to reach the portal, and start running desperately along the road. The host of the Dead do, in fact, gallop after them, almost catching up with them.

Then each of the girls throws a shoe, and then the other . . . and then the pretty little apron . . .

The Dead slake their hatred momentarily upon those clothes; their crackling fingers tear them up and their grinding teeth rip them mechanically.

Then the pursuit recommences.

The vast vault of the black sky, embroidered with stars, gave the impression of a funerary drape above the shroud of snow extended over the dormant plain.

The haggard eyes of the fugitives also saw, running in front of them, the convulsed silhouettes of bushes.

And on their heels sounded the footfalls of the abominable and eccentric horde.

They threw their skirts and their delicately worked koschula, and their rosaries and their holy medals. Finally, they reached their hata, half expiring of horror, and also of cold.

Then, as one of them bolted the door, they heard an inexpressible voice say:

"You're saved, beauties, you're saved . . . but it isn't befitting that you remain long among the living, after having witnessed the Passover of the Dead."

And, in fact, they did not remain long.

They did not get out of the bed where a fever caused by the fear and cold of that lugubrious night threw them, shivering.

Two weeks later, they both died and went to join the other dead in the cemetery.

Thus they expiated having offended by their presence the Mystery of the Dead: the solemn and redoubtable Mystery of the Dead.

PROSE POEMS
AND
VIGNETTES

BALLADE

To Georges Bellenger

I

IN the perfume of violets, rose and acacias—they encountered one another one morning.

Next to her slightly-open bodice slept roses less sweet than her breasts—and her eyes, which resembled two black violets embalmed like spring.

Rapid are the hours of amour.

One evening, under the stars, she said to him: "I am yours forever."

And the stars betrothed them—the mocking and cold stars.

In the perfume of violets, roses and acacias.

Rapid are the hours of amour.

One day he left, as the little acacia flowers were snowing—

Putting great white patches on the desolate grass, like shrouds
Where butterflies came to die.

II

Are there, then, perfumes that kill?
Once only he breathed the tenebrous flower of her hair,
Once only.
And he forgot the blonde child he had encountered one morning,
In the perfume of violets, roses and acacias.

O the unreal nights, the marvelous nights!
The intoxicating mortal caresses,
The kisses that have the taste of the Dream.
And the languors sweeter than sensuality.
O the unreal nights, the marvelous nights!

An attenuated musk haunted her alcove.
Are there, then, perfumes that kill?

She said: I will only love you—the traitress.
And her unforgettable body had the movements of a beautiful tame animal,
Of a beautiful and dangerous animal—tamed.

One day he found her lips mute and sulky.

Oh, but still with that same taste of the Dream—
mortally intoxicating.

Lips as cruel and mute as perfumed roses, which attract but do not return kisses.

It is in vain that he weeps more than on the day when his mother was laid in the tomb.

The eyes of the beloved have a gaze colder than the marble of mausolea.

And her lips, her lips so dear, remain as mute as roses.

Are there, then, perfumes that kill?

The beautiful and dangerous animal he thought tamed, had eaten his heart in play.

Then he cursed the azure of the sky and the scintillating stars.

He cursed the immutable light of the moon, the song of birds,

And the foliage that whispers mysteriously and perfidiously when appeasing night approaches.

III

But the human heart is forgetful and infidel,

And cursing is very sad when the season of young calices is reborn,

And breezes as tender as kisses.

He remembers the blonde child who said to him one
evening under the stars: "I am yours forever."
And he came back.

But she had gone to sleep in the cemetery,
In the perfume of violets, roses and acacias.

25 November 1882.

WINDOWS
(*Le Capitan*, 1883)

ALONG the boulevards and along the streets they star the houses;

In the gray hour of the morning, folding their shutter-wings, they shelter the exquisite and muffled idleness of the darkness of chilly Dream.

But the sun enables them to blossom like flowers, with their white, red or roseate curtains,

Along the boulevards and along the streets

And while the pane mirrors like dormant water, what disquieting charm and what mute confidences between the pleats of the white, red or roseate curtains!

The arabesques of guipures sing of happy existences,

The joyous fires in the hearth,

The rare flowers with perfumes conveyors of forgetfulness,

The hospitable armchairs in which voluptuous dreams slumber and—in the splendor of frames—the evocations of dreamlands.

But how they weep, the lamentable tattered muslin curtains;

What plaints and what anguish in the scrap of dirty percale that resembles a shroud;

And how tragic are windows devoid of curtains,

Windows as empty as blind eyes,

Where, stuck on the broken pane, pieces of paper plaster over livid scars.

Sometimes, however, it is radiant, the poor window, on the edge of the roof

When, to hide its sad nudity, the sky has painted it all in blue;

With its pot of paltry geraniums, the poor window on the edge of the roof then resembles a fragment of the azure in which flowers are growing;

Along the boulevards and along the streets, they star the houses.

And when the sun sets on its blazing pyre, splashing the horizon with gold and blood,

They are resplendent, like armor

Until the distressing hour when, in the meditation of all objects, obscurity falls, like black snow, in flakes.

*

Then all the reflections are extinguished; all the colors are confounded and effaced;

Only the windows of churches, illuminated by some solitary lamp, radiate softly, mysterious and symbolic.

But it will soon wake up, noctambulatory Paris;

It will open its millions of gas-jet eyes,

And in the turbulent and frenetic evening atmosphere, the windows revive

Along the boulevards and along the streets.

The lamp suspends its familiar globe, a mild sun that enables the intimate hours to blossom;

The candles of chandeliers reflect their joyful clusters in mirrors, like marvelous fruits,

And over the window, which is opal, one sees fugitive shadows glide, to the rhythm of music vaguer than breaths;

Nearby, the windows of houses under construction open like yawns of perpetual ennui;

Under the eaves, the poor candle shivers,

The gas-jet injects its riotous light into the entresols of restaurants, showing the end of a red banquette with gilded nails.

And lamps, candlesticks, candelabra and gas-jets confound their disparate notes in a symphony of radiance,

In which the radiant cantilena of blessed hours mingles with the howling voice of false gaieties,

In which the sounds of celebrations and the sounds of kisses mingle with the gasps of solitary agonies and the clamors of lugubrious debauchery.

Then the silent and cold hour comes to extinguish lights and sounds.

Only the regular tread of a *sergent de ville* goes back and forth on the sonorous sidewalk under the windows, which fall asleep like weary eyes

Along the boulevards and along the streets.

A ROMANCE IN THE MOON
Poem in Prose
(*La Libre Revue*, January 1884)

HE was a poet tormented by a strange disease;

He lived without desires, without ambitions, without jealousy and without joy;

Ignorant of tears sweeter than honey and mortal kisses;

For one evening, full of ecstasy and serenity, he had perceived *in the Moon* the woman he loved with a unique amour;

He had perceived the luminous fiancée who appealed to him with a blue smile.

Destinies had cursed that dreamer. And it was with the disgust of a sick man that he struggled for the exceedingly stale bread and the exceedingly adulterated wine every day.

But when evening came, he forgot the struggle and his long nauseas; and, leaning on his window sill, he sang songs full of amour and superhuman clarity to the luminous fiancée who appealed to him with a blue smile.

The daughters of the Earth dazzled him in vain with the white lightning of their amorous breasts;

In vain they prowled around him with their eyes full of promises;

He remained faithful to the fiancée he had perceived in the Moon, who appealed to him with a blue smile.

He lived thus for many years, awaiting the hour of the eternal hymen;

Then, one evening, full of ecstasy and serenity, he died, the poet tormented by that strange disease.

And his soul flew away, singing a hymn of joy, up there, to the dreamed land, into the arms of the beloved who had appeared to him for such a long time with a blue smile.

And in an alcove made of radiance, intoxicated by amour, he embraced forever his luminous fiancée;

And they loved one another for a long time, a very long time,

With an amour as limpid as the ether, devoid of anxieties, devoid of anguish, devoid of jealousy and devoid of tears.

But one evening, the poet leaned on his window sill as before, and gazed at the Earth . . . with regret.

RUSSIAN LEGEND
(*Le Figaro*, 6 May 1893)

THE prince, the young prince as handsome as a king, is mortally wounded.

While he was hunting in the depths of the woods—O the distracted hunter, distracted by the unique haunting of golden tresses, the heavy golden tresses of the princess, his wife—he was attacked by a malevolent wild boar that wounded him with its sharp fangs.

And now, here he is, as pale as a sprig of jasmine, lying on the bloody brocades of the bed.

Of the fortunate bed where, a few weeks before, he had received the virginal spouse, his princess with the golden hair.

Around the bed, three weeping women are standing: the mother, the sister and the wife.

"Let us run," says the mother, "let us run quickly to the magician who lives wild in the depths of the woods.

"He alone can compose a balm that will cure my handsome prince, as handsome as a king."

When they had reached the depths of the woods, the magician said to them:

"I can cure the young prince; I can give you a balm that will cure the young prince, but in order to pay me for that incomparable balm, it is necessary to give me: you, the mother, your entire right arm; you, the sister, the white hand with the ring on the finger; and you, the wife, the heavy golden tress."

Now they are there, the three weeping women around the dead body.

The mother is weeping, sustaining the head of her beloved prince, felled like a fir tree in the woods.

The sister is weeping at the feet of the prince as handsome as a king.

And the wife is weeping next to his heart.

Next to the dead heart that palpitated with such tender amour for her golden tresses.

And at the place where the mother was weeping there emerged a beautiful river with immortal waves, which still flows today.

Where the sister was weeping there was a lively spring.

But where the wife was weeping there was a little pool, which the first sunlight dried up.

PINK HEATHER
(*La Fronde*, 8 July 1898)

CLAUDIE, who is known as Didi, so close is she to the time when her dresses did not pass the knees, went gravely with her cousin Jean to botanize in the pretty wood in the Bois de l'Isle.

You don't know the Bois de l'Isle? Well, too bad for you. It's the nicest wood on the Château-Thierry line; and when, as at this moment, the afternoon sun is shining there above the foliage, and the trees thus appear to be florid with light, one would swear that it is the Sacred Wood where nymphs are going to appear.

Claudie is, moreover, as pretty as a nymph, and her gray muslin dress gives the impression of a spring cloud.

"Is it true, Mademoiselle, that there is a question of your marrying the rich owner of the Château de Luzancy, who is almost obese?"

"Yes Monsieur, it's true, but as I can't do it, they'll see who they're dealing with, and with what wood I warm myself."

"Good—that's my chic little Didi, who gratified me with fine slaps when we played at little wars."

146

"At your service."

Meanwhile the wood becomes bushier.

The pale green of the creepers, which slide along the trees like little waterfalls; the emerald transparency of the branches forming a screen; the turquoise masses of distant thickets and the jewelry of leaves illuminated by the sky reflecting from their multiple surfaces, like as many tiny mirrors, all cause an enchantment to surge forth in the eyes of our strollers.

And Jean, whose young memory retains the imprint of classical studies, dreams of himself as Daphnis and Claudie as Chloe.

While chatting pleasantly, sometimes interrupting themselves for an innocent caress, they have reached a pathway where the moss disappears under an undulation of pink heather.

They are pretty, those light clusters of preciously-sculpted flowers! And the ensemble seems to form soft cushions thrown on the ground in the Oriental style: cushions of silk and velvet embroidered by fays.

"Suppose we stop here?" Jean suggests.

"Do you think so, cousin? We're already late for tea."

When Claudie gets home, a little late, and sets about pouring the tea with a zeal worthy of all eulogies, there is a little cry of admiration among the guests.

"What a charming fantasy!"

"And how well it suits her!"

Anxiously, Claudie darts a glance at the mirror, and sees herself coiffed, like a hamadryad, in pink heather.

THE CHICKEN COOP
(*La Fronde*, 8 July 1898)

WHAT a racket there is in that farmyard, and what a turbulent and undisciplined little society!

The mother hen is using her most quarrelsome voice, visibly annoyed, but the chicks—who are already beginning to lose the egg-yolk color of early infancy and ought to be behaving as reasonable individuals—are paying no heed. They are scattering in all directions, hurrying as if the most urgent affairs are summoning them.

From behind one can see them running, bare-legged, the skirts of their plumage, still too short, tucked up.

They give the impression of ballet-dancers in pink leotards scurrying with light steps.

The other chickens, spinsters, free of any disturbance, are pecking the ground, unhurriedly, serenely; and the white cock, full of disdain, is parading his boastful crest in the midst of his servile people.

But here comes the farmer's young wife, who is bringing the mash in a bucket, and a charivari ensues, all the more marvelous because she has not been able to prevent the three kids from following her. Here they are, padding barefoot in the straw and filth, jostling one another and mingling their shocks of bushy hair with the plumage of the poultry—so much and so well that the dog Tom—who is warming himself in the sun, his four paws in the air—feels obliged to bay deafeningly, in order to bring everyone to order.

THE POPPY FIELD
(*La Fronde*, 8 July 1898)

A path through the fields, a path running like a peaceful stream between enchanted banks.

Wheat, already inclined under the precious weight of the grain; sainfoin powdered with ink, and blue-tinted rye.

But here is a consternating marvel: a field of wild poppies.

It is like a joyous conflagration. Then, at closer range, the detail of corollas that one might think mouth-to-mouth.

It is laughing, crying with delight; it sounds like a fanfare of matinal cockerels.

Then it is a jewel-case of exasperated rubies, perhaps stolen at the price of blood—splashed blood . . .

Under the delicate breeze, it flutters, crimson butterflies, in a frisson of petals above svelte downy stems.

An opiate aroma emanates from the little black hearts of the poppies, agrarian brothers of the maleficent species.

It would be good to go to sleep in that perfume and amid the violent light of carmined flowers, the light of a stained-glass window in which some primitive master evoked a scene of martyrdom.

"Isn't it a pity to leave a field in such a state, eh?"

That is my proprietor, Monsieur Paul, who is criticizing his neighbor, Père Thomas, to whom that treasure more dazzling than a king's mantle belongs.

"Can you believe that he has that vermin, those evil weeds, in his fields? Oh, the bad cultivator! One can see that he'd rather spend his time in the tavern than at work."

Evil weeds—those marvels that are simultaneously laughing and amorous lips, fire, rubies and blood!

I draw away, indignant against Monsieur Paul, taking away the illusion that if Père Thomas is a drunkard, he is also a poet.

THE AMERICAN UNCLE
(*La Fronde*, 22 July 1898)

PIERRE QUEVILLY had quit the pretty Norman village of Totes, where he had been born, while young, in order to seek his fortune in the United States.

It was in the wake of a quarrel with his only sister, on the subject of the house with its apple orchard, their petty wealth, which it would be necessary to share after their father's death.

And he had found fortune; it appears that one could still find it in those days.

However, he had taken his time. Departed in 1872, while a kind of moral convalescence, after the cruel shocks of the war, rendered the mildness of calm more flavorsome, he came back in 1897. Six hundred thousand francs, which he brought back in more than ten wads of thousand-franc bills when leaving the country, almost consoled him for the supplement of twenty-five years added to the thirty he had had on embarkation; but he had never consoled himself for the homeland:

Those tender hills, bushy with verdure, wallowing idly in the sun like beautiful ruminants, whose pelts, made of forests, would have frissons of ease!

Those blissful valleys softly carpeted with long grass, like a profound agrarian litter in which the life of animals and people is a constant lush morning!

The houses, ribbed with beams, the smoke of which adds moving clouds to the more distant clouds of the sky, seeming to harmonize their healthy respiration with the days that pass in that privileged country.

Of all that Pierre Quevilly retained a delightful memory, which was exalted by absence.

The sister quit in annoyance had died several years before, the early widow of a sedate local innkeeper; she left a son.

That nephew was hardly running around in the memory of the rich farmer, whom nothing had been able to attach to Yankee soil, and who promised himself copious family joys on his return.

Oh, it would not be petty cares and spoiling that his old age would lack. Think about it: a rich uncle!

The idea of a belated marriage attracted him momentarily, but he did not settle upon it.

It's disturbance and bother in the house, he said to himself. A wife would only complain and scold, spoiling the blissful peace to which he aspired above all.

His family would be that of his nephew, who must now be married, and the happy uncle would find bambinos ready-made to cajole.

In the omnibus that took him from Saint Victor to Totes, while a miraculous sunset rendered the surrounding countryside similar to a basket of roses, he thought about all that.

It was bizarre, all the same, not to have seen, and not yet to have spoken to that relative who summarized all the family that Pierre had at present.

Is he even a good fellow?

The idea of an excellent joke suddenly germinated in the mind of the American uncle: to arrive without warning, without making himself known, in the inn kept by that nephew, who must surely have succeeded his father, and to observe his future family at close range before deciding anything.

In the large room where a fine long fire is blazing, before which poultry is roasting, Pierre Quevilly is sitting, deceiving his hunger with draughts of cider.

It does not matter that they are taking a long time to serve the meal. It is bad luck to have arrived on a day of major maneuvers.

All the gilded chickens, shiny with grease, are going to the officers' tables, and he is hungry, especially amid those engaging aromas.

If you knew, my lad, who is sitting at this table, the malign uncle says to himself, *you wouldn't treat him like a negligible client.*

He can see that nephew from behind, at the moment, uncorking champagne. Thickset, on legs enlarged for the effort of the corkscrew, he rather gives the impression of a degenerate elephant, and his hair, thick and short over the massive neck, makes his head seem obstinate and obtuse. When he turns round, Uncle Quevilly thinks that he does not have a good face. Little gray eyes, cunning and suspicious, dark eyelids with circumspect creases, the mouth unfurnished.

Nor is he very amiable, observes the uncle, when the innkeeper responds to his requests that: "It's necessary to serve the messieurs first."

Pierre Quevilly casts an eye over his traveling clothes, and recognizes that he is not flamboyant.

Nevertheless, he lacks flair, the nephew. Ah, here's his wife coming in from the garden with the fruit. She isn't beautiful either, and a good dozen years older than her husband. Evidently a rational marriage.

A stout housewife, her bosom hanging down casually under her camisole, her aggressive eyes behind discolored eyebrows, her jaw slack too, in the Norman fashion.

Pierre Quevilly is shocked, in his habits of Yankee correctness, but above all he is dying of hunger, and he hails the waitress impatiently—a pretty maidservant, in truth, who is rushed off her feet and does not know which way to turn.

Meanwhile, the nephew communicates his impressions to his wife.

"If that old man over there asks for a room"—he indicates the American uncle—"tell him that they're all taken by the soldiers. I don't remember that bird—who knows where he's come from?"

At present, Pierre Quevilly, finally served, is eating heartily and gazing complaisantly at Catherine, the waitress with plump arms, who also resembles something good to eat, with her cheeks like rosy apples.

Good! It will please him to shell out now!

✻

"So, you have nothing to give me in order to sleep to-night?"

"Nothing at all, and you won't find anything else-where."

"You might try at the tobacconist's," suggests Catherine.

"In this rain, who'd want to set foot outside?"

"I'll go and see," purrs Catherine.

"No, my girl," the proprietor replies to her. "I need you here to serve the coffee."

"So you'll leave me to sleep under the stars on a night like this!" said Uncle Pierre indignantly.

"Well, I don't see any remedy, unless you go back to the station, but you risk missing the train to Rouen."

In fact, Pierre Quevilly, after having paid the bill, vis-ibly inflated, for his meal at the inn, took two hours to return to the station by patache, in the rain, where he missed the last train and decided to wait on a bench until daylight, at least under shelter.

It was a fantastic night: drowsiness disturbed by the passing of express trains, which gave the illusion of an earthquake and the end of the world; semi-slumbers in which the silhouette of Catherine moved, becoming and agreeable, and the surly, inhospitable mask of the nephew became more hideous, with an urgent and hypocritical grimace, on learning of his relationship with the rich traveler, an old bachelor.

✳

Pierre Quevilly bought land in Totes, had a luxurious and comfortable house constructed there, which queened the pawn of the entire neighborhood, and married Catherine.

I can assure you that on discovering the truth and the terrible gaffe they had committed, the nephew and his wife put on a filthy expression, effortlessly.

THE PLEDGE
(*La Fronde*, 26 August 1898)

IT is their last rendezvous in the little guard-house, which the young gentleman has been visiting for eight months in order to meet his humble friend. Tomorrow, he is returning to Paris.

Little Rose, who loves him so much, is chilled by chagrin, but dare not speak for fear of saddening these supreme moments.

She had known such powerful joys in belonging to him. At first there had only been an ardent pride at being distinguished—her, a simple peasant—by the handsome lord with the white hands, who spoke so softly and whose garments smelled good. Then, all of her vigorous virgin blood, grown in the fields like a supple poplar, sang like spring-water set over a big fire.

She was the amorous bacchante and the frolicsome mistress and the twittering little bird and the confident little spouse, forgetting the abyss open between them, sensing her heart melt with tenderness and her eyes moisten with happy tears.

She was not unaware that he would leave one day; but in that dolor worse than death she still savored an exaltation of a martyr expiring for her faith.

Now, this week, she has sensed that she will be a mother.

He, meanwhile, had found delicate sensations in that savage flirtation.

The odor of resin and sweet marjoram exhaled by the coarse cloth in which the agrarian beauty of Rose is enveloped, her heavy hair the color of harvests, undulating like the water of the river, her eyes in which light and dark play, as amid the foliage of willows, all had a savor quite different from banal adventures in Parisian boudoirs: music-hall performers inflated with vanity and stupidity, coarsely venal courtesans playing the comedy of passion without talent, and bored socialites.

But he is of that exhausted race himself, where the wellspring of emotions rapidly runs dry; and now he is weary of his rural passionette.

He departs without regret, with the memory of a fresh, warm and agreeable scent, as when one crushes a sprig of mint between distracted fingers.

"Adieu, Rose; think of me sometimes."

She makes no response.

People in the country are not kind to a girl who has fallen, and Rose has to support cruel words and cruel smiles with resignation.

Her aged father cannot bear them; he has gone to join his worthy wife in the cemetery behind the church, where he will be very comfortable, It is such a pretty cemetery, on a hill, and when the sun is shining it seems

to be laughing peacefully with all those bright stones—
laughing at the living who agitate for such little things,
for so few hours—while the birds make a delightful din
there in the bushes.

Rose's child is born.

A charitable old woman who lives on the edge of the
forest, who is said to be a little mad, helps the poor young
woman abandoned by everyone else. And when she
brings to the mother's bed the child that she is holding
with precaution in her trembling and unskillful hands,
Rose weeps and sobs and laughs.

"The Lord be blessed; I haven't lost him entirely."

AMOROUS SIESTA
(*La Fronde*, 26 August 1898)

THE summer afternoon pours a milky light through the rural muslin curtains, and the foliage of the garden mingles glaucous reflections with it, as in a submarine palace.

Nelly and Jacques, abandoned limply in the hollow of a divan, are doubtless savoring an unforgettable moment, sweeter than the excitement of embraces: a weary inebriation made of fulgurant intoxications.

Their hands have found one another without searching, and they both sense their hearts living precisely in the other loving heart.

Two successful human specimens:

She, tall and slim, but not thin, with soft chestnut hair, her face refined by an interesting neurosis, supple and fresh of complexion: he, blond in the eyes and the hair, with energetic features, with a flavorsome mouth.

The chirping of birds comes from the garden.

Syringas in vases exhale an innocent and perverse perfume, as complex as the sensuality of a kiss stolen by surprise.

What are they thinking while their embrace is mute?

Overwhelmed by an excess of bliss, they surely feel sorry for the rest of humankind, who waste a brief existence in vain agitations, for want of knowing this unique wealth: mutual tenderness?

Or perhaps, sensing themselves so happy, they fear the revenge of Fatality?

It might be that beneath the benediction of a superhuman felicity, their hearts—already brushed by chilling social life and its skepticism—are returning to the candor of primary beliefs and confident in the protection of Heaven and the fragile treasure of their amour?

Well, no.

She is thinking, with a signal bitterness about her dearest childhood friend, who has stolen her husband.

He is haunted by the vision of his only child, dead of the despair of the mother, who collapsed at the moment when she discovered the treason.

The chirping of birds comes from the garden . . .

The summer afternoon pours a milky light through the rural muslin curtains . . .

MARTHE
(*La Fronde*, 26 August 1898)

MARTHE drops the book in which her attention is striving in vain and consults the clock mechanically.

Two o'clock!

These desolate nights have already been her life for months.

From the evening when she acquired the proof of the treason and, finally, Léonce's own confession, each of her late nights has brought its lot of refined and varied dolors, following a regular progress, like a physical illness, with its crescendo of suffering, its phase of prostration, and the crisis in which the decision is vehemently affirmed to break with everything, to extract herself from these tortures . . . and then the poor harassed heart falls back into the cowardice of acceptance.

Tonight, however, the decision grows in Marthe's mind, shored up by a revolt of the administration of justice.

By what right have her ardent thirty years been put out to pasture, disdained by a man who has become incapable of caring about her?

Oh, Lord, must there also be the danger of becoming an old woman before her time? No, it's necessary to put an end to it. It's necessary to save herself, as from a house on fire, from this house deserted by love.

Is not amour the beauty and youth of every woman?

Finally, like an invalid extenuated in a slumber full of dreams, Marthe falls into delightful memories of the early days of the marriage. Reminiscences pass incoherently, in shreds: ecstatic walks on beaches illuminated by their joy; worldly triumphs when, leaning on the arm of the beloved, she provoked a murmur of admiration, without it being able to embarrass her, so beautiful with joy did she sense herself to be.

Then, O cruelty! The passionate minutes surge forth with phantom words of flame and the mirage of gazes transfigured by amorous delirium.

It is another who now possesses his emotions, by which she was once intoxicated. Oh, in one who was once so close!

So Marthe no longer wants that insult. Life is not finished at her age. She will recommence her life. Her enervation is doubled by the impatient desire from a definitive explanation, which she will have this very evening, or she will signify her unbreakable determination to separate.

The noise of every carriage that passes by makes her shiver, and makes bellicose blood flow to her cheeks. And when the noise draws away and fades away, like a sea unfurling over shingle, disappointment grips her like a ferocious clawed hand.

Suddenly, her heart is traversed by a sharper pain on hearing three o'clock chime, Léonce has never returned so late; it isn't natural . . . Some accident has befallen him . . . ! Oh, Léonce is dead!

All her tortured body begins to tremble as if in a great chill. And that chill now suppresses all thought, by virtue of being a supreme and absorbing Gehenna—when Léonce comes in, tranquilly.

With an exquisite egotism, he is accustomed to the apparent resignation of his wife, having no suspicion of her storms and lacerations

"Still up at this hour, my dear?" he says, yawning.

"Yes, I was reading a curious book."

And as they have kept, from the early years of their marriage, the habit of sleeping in the same bed, as soon as he is undressed, he falls asleep, while Marthe, next to him—poor Marthe!—feels completely glad to know that he is there, alive . . . and to be less cold.

MORNING
(*La Fronde*, 17 September 1898)

IT is positively as if one were sticking one's nose in a bouquet, that first step into the country, in the morning.

In the middle of the courtyard, the heap of straw, in slack sheaves, exhales a warm odor of haymaking.

From the garden, where the roses and the resedas do not disdain to fraternize with the potatoes, the cabbages and the sorrel, comes a mingled perfume, innocent and warm.

The flowers of the pumpkins light little Japanese lanterns under the ample screens of the geranium leaves, igniting fireworks to amuse the carrots, whose foliage is precious lace perforated with great care. The children of a king are not better clad at such an early hour. Even the onions, as poorly groomed and ragged as four sous, are weeping with chagrin.

And the orchestra!

It is varied, I beg you to believe.

The cows, modulate a broad chant as they walk, in a profound contralto. The cock responds peremptorily.

A dog joins in; he has a slight altercation with a passer-by of nasty appearance.

As for the family of sparrows, there is a series of misunderstandings, which will never be cleared up, and arguments that will never end. Perhaps there are questions of inheritance or shared branches.

Let us go a little way along the road.

Look, all the trees have already woken up, and are blinking their thousand green eyelids in the sunlight, with a soft sound of welcome. One might think it the rustle of little waterfalls.

The houses also have their shutters open, and here, in the depths of a vegetable garden, a young peasant-woman is nursing her baby, as pink and gilded as a freshly-picked fruit.

MULBERRIES
(*La Fronde*, 17 September 1898)

LUCAS and Colinette are returning from the commissions they have executed for their parents in the nearby village.

They are engaged to be married in mid-October.

What a pretty route they are following at the moment!

To the left there is the entrance to the bushy wood: oaks, elms, alders and firs

The foliage is so dense that if the eyes can sometimes distinguish an interruption, it seems to be looking into a dark cave in the profound shadow.

To the right, a living hedge entangles its thorns, its wild roses and its brambles, the long, clawed branches of which hang down all the way to the road, embroidered with elegant foliage in green stars. Oh, here are myriads of mulberries, in tempting clusters, mulberries in profusion.

But they do not yet have the desirable maturity; that's a pity.

Instead of being black they have a delicate coral hue, which greatly resembles Colinette's lips.

And they shine in the sunshine, as if molded in light, extending amid the branches like full baskets presented gracefully . . .

In places, at distant intervals, a fruit is beginning to turn violet, and Colinette picks it with squeals of joy so genteel and so gay, so similar to the chirping of sparrows that respond to them, that Lucas, either out of tenderness or greed, in order also to have a little of the ripening mulberry, kisses his friend's pretty lips.

But Colinette pushes him away tenderly.

"We might as well wait for the curé's permission; it won't be long now."

And when, in a month's time, they come back as husband and wife to the hedge covered in ripe fruits, like offerings, they will have a regret for that mild day when it was necessary to search for mulberries ready for picking, which hid, and they avoided caresses stolen by surprise.

GREEN APPLES
(*La Fronde*, 17 September 1898)

MONSIEUR JOSEPH, who has long been known as "the widower," or, more recently, as "the old man," lives alone in his enclosure. He is not seen traversing the village three times a year.

Sober and undemanding, he nourishes himself from his garden: his potatoes, his lettuces, his carrots and his cabbages, which he cooks himself on his little stove in the entrance, suffice for him. Whitewashed, that entrance is as white as a young woman's bedroom; its narrow window overlooks the orchard and the widower takes his daily walk there when he is not tending his field.

It is not that he is more miserly than anyone else, or poorer. On the contrary; he has wealth, and the neighbors who have daughters to marry squint in the direction of his house, and send their demoiselles on various pretexts, sometimes with one commission and sometimes another.

But the old man receives them glacially on his doorstep without even opening the brass wire grille of the door.

To be so grim, does that widower retain a delicate memory of his late wife, and is he able, better than many refined people, to enclose himself in a faithful melancholy, which he cherishes?

Nothing of the sort.

He had a very poor relationship with his wife, who was, to tell the truth, shrewish and as quarrelsome as a red hen. And it is precisely for that reason that Monsieur Joseph cannot weary of savoring his reconquered independence, applauding his fortunate widowhood. It would require a clever woman to bring him back to the Mairie.

There was also a little adventure in Monsieur Joseph's youth that weighs upon his memory and is not made to reconcile him with the feminine tribe, to which he willingly refers as the seductive sex.

He was smitten with Mademoiselle Louise, a young maidservant at the château, who was blonde and white and as plump as a quail. He wanted to marry her without a valiant sou. You can imagine what a bad way he was in.

But it was Mademoiselle Louie who was proud, and did not want a peasant. She departed one day with her masters' coachman, sacked because of who knows what machinations with the oats.

Monsieur Joseph had never consoled himself completely for that disappointment. And after his marriage, which was a furnace of a different kind, he enveloped women with a general reprobation compounded, in sum, of wounded sensibility.

Monsieur Joseph is not so very old; he is approaching his fifty-second year, and in order that his blood of a robust fellow does not give him any bad advice, he has his daily comings and going to all the corners of his orchard and his field, and a constant war against wasps, caterpillars and weeds—everything required to procure beneficial fatigue and to enable him to sleep the slumber of the innocent at night.

This afternoon, the widower perceives a little girl from his window, under the big apple tree. How has the satanic little wretch got in? It must be through the hole in the hedge that he has forgotten to fill in.

Hoisting herself up on the toes of her clogs, she is taking hold of the lowest branches and picking the apples, which she crunches with small click of solid teeth, stuffing herself hastily.

She is not a local child. She must be a gipsy brat. She might be fifteen years old, but she is very thin.

It might be the case that she does not eat every day, and is hungry.

The apples were not even ripe, damn it! But they are as green as gooseberries and as hard as bricks.

Under the dark shock of tousled hair, two lovely dark eyes, searching and busy, laughing and defiant, in a sun-tanned face that is still childish, but two living apples, round and small—not yet ripe—protrude beneath the coarse chemise.

From hay stored under the hangar an intoxicating odor rises that blends with that of plants still vivacious but already attenuated by the autumn: plants pearled by recent rain, which exhale scents as expressive as words.

The widower falls into mild languor. An autumn dew is also rising in his heart and his eyes fraternal to those vegetal emanations at the decline of the season in which sap ferments into warm incense.

Memories assail him of the time when he loved Mademoiselle Louise, so blonde and so pale.

And the wild child out there—how pretty she is!

Suddenly, Monsieur Joseph bounds to the orchard, shouting: "Get out, damnable breed! And quicker than that, or I'll break your back!"

And he continues to threaten her with his stick as she makes off along the road.

THE BUILDING
(*La Fronde*, 17 September 1898)

THE old building is there, amid the cheerful verdure, sprawling and weary, like an animal close to its end.

The walls are slightly split everywhere, the windows holed here, completely destroyed there, and stopped up with straw and planks.

The thatch of the roof is blackened, as if escaped from a fire.

The palisade at the entrance, where ivy is still climbing again and thorns falling outside, is uprooted, and one can see the abandoned courtyard, with hay trailing in the midst of thistles.

A superb pear tree shades that decrepitude, and when the sun shines, all of that becomes smiling, tenderly resigned.

It is no longer the image of a sudden death endured with resistance, but merely a peaceful end to things, a descent into sleep in the bosom of the great calm of nature.

A poor old man emerges from the ruined building and goes to lie down, like a lizard, on the grass, avoiding the shadow of the pear tree in order not to lose any of the benevolent warmth.

His garments are the same color as the worm-eaten planks; too large, they float over an emaciated body from which a lugubrious cough emerges; the old peasant is dying slowly in his crumbling house.

Ah! A visitor for the old man.

A cart that has come via the road to Gros Rouvre stops in front of the house. A solid fellow gets down, with a pretentiously attired middle-aged woman.

It is the son of the daughter-in-law of the owner of the building—innkeepers established in Gros Rouvre

Before even a bonjour, the woman says: "It's very ill, very ill," examining the cracked walls.

"Well, how goes it, Father?" asks the son, gaily.

"It's . . . it's fine," coughs the old man.

"That house is in dire need of repair; it's hardly holding up, and will fall down one of these days."

"Bah!" gasps the old man. "We'll live as long as one another."

"But if it's allowed to fall down," the woman objects, "the land won't be worth much."

"Yes," says the innkeeper, "but the repairs would cost dear; it's all out of alignment, the house; it would be necessary to push it back. It's a lot of building work, and a lot of expense."

"That's annoying, on the one hand," drones the woman, "but what if it falls on the old man?"

"Bah! We're all mortal," the son philosophizes. "Better to let it."

And as the old man, who has not understood very well, nods his head vaguely, his children climb back into the cart and the son cries to him, while enveloping the horse with a crack of the whip:

"*Au revoir*, Father! Look after yourself!"

THE PEARS
(*La Fronde*, 23 September 1898)

OLD ROGUINE, renowned in the village for her avarice and her egotism, went down into her orchard one morning.

"Good God of fate! Thieves! Thieves again!"

Pears are missing from several trees.

It is not that a few pears more or less is a great crime.

She lives alone, having never been married, and she was able to send to the devil the children of a sister who died abroad and who came to find her when they were repatriated to France.

Where would it end if it were necessary to occupy oneself with all sorts of unfortunates, relatives or not?

In years of abundance she could sell her fruit in the city, but the railway station is a long way away, there is no service and no connection, and there would be more expense than profit.

All the same, that is no reason why people should steal her property.

It would be necessary to raise the fence—but that would mean more expense.

Suddenly, a luminous idea occurs to her.

Is there not a liter of copper sulfate on a shelf in the kitchen, of which she makes use for scouring?

Every time she renews the provision, the grocer puts a blood-red label on it, and reminds her that it is poisonous.

That is something that might take away the taste for pears from their lovers—and a taste for bread as well.

And while the sun spreads a warmth as caressant as a maternal bosom, ready to welcome all the motherless, and all the homeless, while the generous radiance ripens the heavy gifts of autumn on the branches for those without bread, the Megaera sprinkles her pears with copper sulfate.

The next day she is astonished to learn that vagabonds have died in the hospice, having been picked up agonizing on the road, and that her good neighbor the watchman—oh, the little wretch—has died in the midst of his family, also writhing in the torments of poison.

STORMY WEATHER
(*La Fronde*, 23 September 1898)

"YOU'LL never be mine."

"Never."

"I know it. But do you love me, Berthe?"

"Yes, I love you, Joe, more than my soul."

"As for me, I cherish you a thousand times more than my life, such that I wouldn't want to renounce a single one of the dolors that come to me from you."

"For me to appear in your eyes, for a single instant, less worthy of your suffering amour, would seem to me to be a more frightful misfortune than the scorn of the whole world."

"And it's thus that I want you, beloved: inaccessible and tormenting, a source of distress and ecstasy."

Through the three large open windows of the room where the lovers were, the park was visible in the splendor of its foliage; but the sky, as pure a little while ago as a child's gaze, has become as pale as an invalid. The crowns of the chestnut trees are oscillating, as if stupefied by hearing some strange story in the rising wind.

Berthe holds her friend's hand and thinks that if, as an ignorant child of sixteen, she had not allowed herself to be married to the man who insults and neglects her, Joe, her beloved, might be her husband.

"What a paradise our life would be then," Joe replies, hearing her thought . . .

A host of black clouds has run from the occident like a flock of evil eagles; the sky is completely obscured by them. In the distance, a growling is audible, similar to that of a captive wild beast.

Berthe and Joe have let go of one another's hands; a malaise is electrifying them, torturing them and making their gazes almost ashamed. But a violent detonation, in which worlds seem to be collapsing, throws the fearful amorous woman back toward that protective strength nearby, the lover, who reassures her with a burning pressure of the hand.

Through a rip in the firmament, a sulfurous light radiates, which causes groups of consternated trees to surge forth, in a spectral attitude

An ambiguous and stagnant atmosphere oppresses the nerves,

Lightning strikes make the air tremble.

But the intervals of calm carry an even more disconcerting asphyxia.

And in the meantime, the jostled branches whisper and mock; the two lovers, without thought, are vanquished by a quivering and cowardly humanity. They sense a fraternity with all that bewildered nature . . . their embrace becomes as unavoidable as the crisis of the elements, and their lips join with the profound and deafening clamor of clouds colliding in the storm.

At present, enlaced, they weep for a long time, while in the park, dense and heavy raindrops descend upon the fallen leaves.

THE PLUMS
(*La Fronde*, 23 September 1898)

"WOULD you like to come to pick plums with us in the new field; we're going to make jam with them."

"Of course I'd like to, but I warn you, I'm very greedy; my help will cost you dear."

And we set forth, Monsieur and Madame Charles, the owners, my friend Jeanne and I, for the new field, each with a basket over the arm. The sun of the finishing afternoon seems to have found a position that pleases it, which it will maintain for some time without changing.

The fields, the paths and the trees have the charity of a naïve, overly precise image.

The path underfoot allows a thin, low dust to rise, from which shoes emerge like thieves, and when we take a short cut through a meadow, the grass rustles as it lies down and immediately springs up again, brushed by skirts.

Finally, here are the plum trees with meager foliage punctuated with little green balls.

There are a great many on the ground, ravaged by wasps, some of which buzz when they are disturbed.

Monsieur Charles—a good fellow, thickset and strong in his canvas trousers—has taken off his jacket and his muscles are bulging under the wool; he stirs the branches with a pole, and a thick hail falls upon our straw hats, pattering on shoulders, backs and everywhere.

Well, no one any longer has a desire to eat any of them; a competitive zeal takes possession of the ladies as to who will fill her basket most rapidly with the most beautiful plums.

They are cool to the touch, firm and soft, dusted with a fine powder, like marquises.[1]

Then it is necessary to run after them, because they roll and steal away slyly, and it is the ugly ones and the stained ones that offer themselves, as if to make fun of you.

All the same, my basket is beginning to feel heavy.

Oof! It ends up becoming tiring. A little halt.

Ah, the excellent repose on the grass! How good the air smells! How silent everything is!

Except for Jeanne, who resumes a story interrupted, it seems, a little while ago; I no longer remember. May the Devil bless her!

It is a matter of a friend, a country neighbor who—can you imagine?—retains her one evening in anticipation of a return of the husband, for there is a replacement hiding in the bedroom. That is what happens, in fact, and my Jeanne finds herself face to face with a lover, whom she has never even seen—the friend's, of course—obliged to

---

1 There is a kind of pear known in France as a marquise; the ambiguity is obviously intentional.

cede a chair in her bedroom to him, in order to save the situation.

The funniest thing is . . .

But I am no longer listening. A good animal languor, devoid of thought, has conquered me.

I merely gaze, without seeing very well, at Madame Charles, standing, with her little paunch rounded like a plum.

She is, I believe, expecting for Christmas.

A herd of milk cows, red, white and as noble as ladies of quality, passes along the road, lowing, and the wind brings a warm and healthy odor.

NORMAN VALLEYS
(*La Fronde*, 3 November 1898)

AFTER all those broad horizons in which the sea stacks its steps of foam as if for ideal ascents; after the saline perfumes of wrack left at low tide on the sculpted sands, engraved with capricious designs by the moving waves, the return to Paris is rather melancholy.

However, the journey on the Norman line is an enchantment.

While the rhythm of the train sings a soft and energetic lullaby, innumerable landscapes are framed in the window of the compartment.

In the beginning, between the houses, the orchards and the meadows, one sees the sea reappearing, more beautiful in that fugitive vision, which seems to be addressing an adieu to you with its vast azure eye.

Then, nothing more except wooded hills, the moist valley suspended like a hammock for happy idleness.

The indolent cows wandering over the meadows group together numerously, with their joyful pelts, on the undulating lawns.

There are brown ones, with the velvety hues of otter-skin and aggressive horns—they are the bad ones, it appears.

Others are bright russet with sentimental eyes, the tufts of their tails swing back and forth like coquettish fans.

Some, white with black and ocher patches, are lying down like huge seashells left by the nearby ocean.

Yet others are as blonde as English misses.

Their hooves caress the grass tenderly; and their profiles are raised ingenuously toward space, with dreamy slowness. The villages with thatched roofs huddled in the verdure resemble other animals, quiet and contented.

Apple trees in the fields, on banks and on the slopes around wooden houses with apparent beams.

Apple trees everywhere.

Apple trees laden with red apples, as if flowering with large roses, or apples as brilliant as new ivory.

The foliage is hardly visible beneath the profusion of fruit.

Some seem to be running impatiently to offer their treasure, others incline, almost kneeling, pliant under the weight. The branches sway in the wind, dangling like garlands.

On the ground, there are fallen apples under every tree, and those corners of grass constellated with gold resemble little ponds in which a starry sky is mirrored.

In the poplars along the route the yellow fruits also give the illusion of ripe fruits.

Here, at a little station, are trains laden with apples, wagons entirely filled with them, all cheerful with sumptuous colors of amber and carmine. There are even some on the track, dispersed on the haste of loading.

The train pulls away again, and there are more hills covered with trees of every species: oaks, firs, elms and poplars, so bushy that at a distance it resembles a high moss dappled with warm autumnal tones.

White villages with church steeples in the middle are stacked on the slopes of hills, as if rising and falling.

The living hedges cling to the autumnal sunlight like as many emerald facets mingled with the foliage of wild roses, dried, rusted and reddened by October, which is putting adornment upon them of artificial roses and illusory flowers.

And always apple trees.

That vainly offered temptation ends up being painful.

A blast of the whistle; the train stops: Lisieux.

Ah! Here is a young indigene, a barefoot Norman gamin, who has had the good idea of bringing a few fruits for the travelers.

Decidedly, that race has a genius for trade.

"How much are your apples?"

"Three francs a basket."

The basket, it is necessary to say, consists of three apples posed on a piece of bark. That makes a franc apiece, and I perceive that two of them are wormy.

"That's a little dear."

"Oh, Madame, it seems that way, but there are not many of them this year."

I still have eyes dazzled by the mad profusion with which the generous autumn has lavished its gifts without bargaining.

So I send the impudent young trader away, and I no longer have any desire for Norman apples.

AUTUMN BEACH
(*La Fronde*, 3 November 1898)

THE wind is blowing without being muffled by a cold drizzle.

On the foggy, vaporous and monotonous horizon, the sea, confounded with the sky, is rising, animated by a muted anger.

The surly waves take on a vehement surge, and then fall back heavily, discouraged, in cascades of wan foam, with the sound of a dive, the sound of a suicide. Other waves respond; one might think it distant cannon fire.

However, every assault of the surf on the beach leaves large festoons of lace and displays trails of precious embroidery that disappear like a flight of fearful nereids.

Jacques and Nelly are walking without speaking, chilled by the drizzle, saddened by the grayness, as implacable as a sword blade.

When they look at one another, a little hatred lights up beneath the eyelashes.

They search for a distraction from their morose humor and discover reciprocal grievances.

It's him who is determined to conclude his affairs before leaving.

It's her who is demanding this voyage in spite of the advanced autumn.

Oh, the egotism of men!

The stubbornness of women!

The decline of the season causes the years lived together, with the inevitable collisions—long illuminated by amour, however—to weigh heavily upon their hearts.

Oh, there's a rainbow. The bad weather won't last long.

And now the sunset is igniting: one of those superb sunsets of which only the months of Ventose and Pluviose can be proud.

A troop of red clouds, a herd of Olympian cows with udders heavy with celestial water, travels before the sun, which inflates them with gold.

Conquering, the arrows of Apollo have rapidly disperses the somber vagabonds; they are light-winged mares now drawing a nacreous chariot florid with delicate violets, in which pink forms stand in attitudes of victory.

The fleecy clouds gather again, traversed by light; and there is the apparition of a suspended landscape, an aerial clearing, with trees crested with pink gold, grouped harmoniously, framed by great mauve willows, which dissolve, leaving a lilac lake striped by fire.

Jacques and Nelly, calmed by those enchantments, sense that the interior life, like the life of the elements, is made of bitterness and sweetness, despair and expansion in beauty, and that it is necessary to support the changed minutes while awaiting the clarifications.

They join their reconciled hands, while a charming line of poetry murmurs in their memory:

"It is necessary, you see, to forgive us things."[1]

The sea, calmer, is liquid sapphire. In the hollows of the waves rose petals float, shredded by the sunset.

---

1 The first line of an oft-quoted poem by Paul Verlaine

DEAD LEAVES
(*La Fronde*, 3 November 1898)

THROUGH the window overlooking the park Geneviève watches—without really seeing—the autumn leaves spiraling.

It is the moment of the season when everything is wounds and detachments: the dramatic clouds splashed the murderous colors, the withering of flowers still on the leaning stems—but where is their spring grace?

The branches maltreated by the wind squeal in pain under the insult.

Later, an icy peace will descend over these rancors, but for the moment, there is a revolted acceptance, a memory still too recent of the flames, the tenderness and the languors of summer.

That faded service tree, how joyfully it laughed—yesterday, it seems—with all its pretty berries, as red as lips, while its branches stretched voluptuously, like enervated arms, over an exquisite sky.

And Geneviève thinks that this season resembles the hour of her life that she has reached.

What had prevented her from perceiving it was Jean's faithful love: that amour to which she has sacrificed for ten years—but with what joy!—the murmurs of her umbrageous conscience, accepting to lie to her husband, and to lie to her child.

Even accepting the remorse of condemning Jean, whose idolater and jealous mistress she is, to an existence without a hearth.

A recent voyage of her friend, which was unexpectedly prolonged, had not given her any anxiety: merely a little melancholy and nostalgia for dear kisses.

And now, by means of a letter—rather dry and offensive—she has learned of her friend's marriage.

Not even a rational marriage: he is marrying an adventuress, who has inflamed his blood, rendered lukewarm by overly familiar caresses.

Geneviève goes to seek in a hiding place a casket, which she opens in front of her.

They are his old letters.

Those dangerous letters, from which she never dared separate herself, preferring a constant anguish, obsession and the dread of dying without having destroyed them.

The raised lid reveals a mirror framed by delicate sculptures in gold and tortoiseshell.

Oh, how she understands the lover's defection.

Her eyes, misted at that moment by tears, are like the autumnal sky regretting its former brightness.

Her lips are tarnished like the berries of the service tree, under which Jean once embraced her, drunk with temerity and passion.

And her dazzling complexion, once like the petals of tea-roses, has also faded, like them.

They are there, Jean's letters.

Without even rereading those pages, on which are inscribed the flames, the tenderness and the languor of the season of amour, Geneviève tears them into tiny pieces and disperses them through the window, on the autumnal wind, in the park, where they go to join the other dead leaves.

NOVEMBER LEAVES
(*La Fronde*, 11 November 1898)

$\mathbf{A}$RE not these faded leaves that the wind crumples mechanically like pages ripped angrily from some book once written by hope and illusion?

A season has sufficed for all sap to dry up and all fervor to be chilled.

"O vase of sadness! O great taciturn!"[1]

How that beautiful line by Baudelaire suits this season crowned by dry branches, the season of All Hallows.

At the foot of the walls that enclose the funereal gardens, life with its agitations unfurls like the sea at the foot of a cliff, vainly attempting the assault. For this is the domain of inviolable peace and dreams without awakening.

I have the memory of a cemetery in Bernay, seen at the same moment of the year.

---

1 From a poem in *Les Fleurs du Mal* whose first line is "Je t'adore à l'égal de la voûte nocturne" [I adore you as much as the nocturnal vault].

The church, posed high on a hill—a very beautiful Henri II church, all in preciously-worked white stone—makes one think of some apocalyptic skeleton, elegant and macabre.

The tombstones on which names and dates are engraved, are grouped in the enclosure like a flock assembled by the shepherd.

The city of the dead overlooks a beautiful Norman valley that shines with all the splendors of autumn.

Here they are, face to face: living Nature with her indefatigable births, her long cares and its fleeting joys, and Death, full of anguishing mystery.

In the rural regions of the north, the separation of the living and the defunct is attenuated.

After the Sunday mass, families spread out among the sepulchers and mingle the genteel sounds of life with the indulgent silence of the tombs. Betrothals receive the sanction of absent parents there.

In Parisian cemeteries the renewed flowers shine like pious candles amid the somber green of cypresses; the dead leaves moan under the melancholy footsteps of visitors.

How many tears, how many emotional reveries commune there with the poor dead—whose solitude is perhaps consoled.

Widows and mothers curse impious Death, and then take refuge in the hope of celestial reunions.

But how tragic the ancient tombs are in their abandonment!

What revolts *shut up* under the earth that covers your hearts of wives, your hearts of lovers—forgotten dead!

And you, child's white tomb! The woman who watered you with so many tears is now rocking a new cradle . . .

Thought is saddened in this décor of declines: the decline of the season . . . the end of destinies.

What is the good of so many puerile struggles? Toward what end is the breathless course of our efforts directed?

As soon as we are outside melancholy doors, here is the suburban quarter with its noisy ginguettes, the naïve rudeness of petty merchants, the newsvendors who offer the scandal of the day for a sou.

And finally, at a street corner, two young lovers who are biting, while laughing, into the same apple.

FIRST FIRES
(*La Fronde*, 11 November 1898)

THROUGH the delicate curtains of embroidered lawn a light enters, chilly, hesitant and tender.

The drawing room with the bright furniture seems lunged thereby in a matinal mist, and the log fire in the hearth lights up like a rising sun.

Claudie, charming and frail in that half-light, sitting at the piano, is singing a melody by Schumann while her cousin Jacques is turning the pages.

He is turning them rather poorly, distracted by a chestnut curl that designs something very nicely on Claudie's delicate nape.

In front of the fire, the good aunt, in a padded arm-chair, seems very interested in the flight of sparks and the changing colors of the flames.

Sometimes, she darts a sly glance at the young couple.

Something like an autumn mist moistens her faded eyes then, which shine nevertheless with joy and hope.

Simply because of the excitement of the young beauty singing the admirable words of Heinrich Heine:

"My eyes wept in a dream."

Simply because of the carmine that makes the tips of Jacques' ears similar to the little crackling flames, the good aunt has understood that Jacques and Claudie adore one another.

"Heaven bless you, dear children, and spare you," she murmurs, and while the logs crumble in the spiraling smoke, her mind reviews the long sequence of her memories, happy and cruel.

Charitably, the good aunt pretends to be asleep, and the young folk immediately take advantage of it to give one another the first kiss of amour, ardent and forceful, without breaking the silence of the room, which seems to be plunged in a matinal mist, brightened, as if by a rising sun, by the glimmer of a first fire of November.

WINTER FLOWERS
(*La Fronde*, 11 November 1898)

HOW melancholy and touching they are, the flowers of winter!

Hothouse roses, devoid of perfume, violets whose odor has expired, lilacs with pale breath.

They are almost the sisters of artificial flowers, flowers of velvet and silk.

Amid the verdure deported of palm trees—for what crime, great God?—a desolate and suffering verdure, they put their plaintive grace, their dream of free air and unknown sunlight.

Flowers in beribboned baskets in the dressing rooms of actresses, in the boudoirs of courtesans, pure and sad flowers, to what complicities is your innocence lent! With what disdain are you thrown, languishing, in the midst of make-up and frippery!

Flowers that wilt amid the warmth of heaters in brightly-lit drawing rooms, where hothouse passions are agitating, without sap and without perfume; where the phantom of Amour grimaces under your heartbroken gazes, phantoms of flowers!

How I prefer you, vivacious chrysanthemums, flowers of the after-season with a savage aroma.

It is thanks to you that the withered garden illuminates with a last light. It is you that furtive fingers attach to the humble corsage in which an authentic emotion palpitates.

It is your tousled plumes that ornament the table on Sunday.

And, placed on the table by a faithful hand, you retain the fresh charm of your colors for a long time.

However, in artful hands they are able to become enchanted flesh, docile and miraculous.

Assembled then in some mundane place, they are a gallery of masterpieces.

The painter and the sculptor admire their subtle tones, sumptuous and delicate, and their fantastic, eloquent forms; the poet recognizes in their nuances and attitudes the diverse soul of flowers. Some are melancholy with dangling petals, some crested with pride, others seductive and thoughtful.

They are also like the apotheosis and the synthesis of the year, like a hymn of praise sung by the winter flowers to all the defunct flowers.

One sees again on the beautiful bosom of chrysanthemums the virginal whiteness of lilies of the valley and the violets of April. The warm roses of summer are mirrored in pink chrysanthemums, and is it not of the rust of autumn woods that those proud clusters are made?

The tones of fruits too: cherry, orange, apricot; the hues of amorous women's dresses.

Those exquisite flowers render us, in the middle of morose winter, the magic of the radiant seasons.

AMOUR AND PSYCHE
(*La Fronde*, 25 November 1898)

CAMILLE fell into Jacques' life just at the right moment.

A big fellow, twenty-five years old, he was taking his first steps of independence, having meekly and dreamily accepted until then the yoke of puritan parents, who had made their son a quasi-demoiselle.

So, liberated a trifle abruptly by a quarrel, Jacques tasted entirely new joys; and his first mistress coincided with the first pleasures of installation in his own home, a true home.

Delighted to be in love, Jacques savored delicately everything that came to him from that liaison.

Camille's hat, placed on his bed, transported him easily, by the evocation of licentious rapprochements.

"Shocking, Madame, your hat on a young man's bed; what can it be doing there?"

Camille knew the price of that sentimental freshness, and delighted in it like a she-cat.

One thing of which Jacques showed himself to be fond was *scenes*.

Camille regaled him with them without counting.

A day spent at Saint-Germain was terminated under a downpour by a refusal on Camille's part to go back, or even to take shelter. Jacques had to agree that *all that* was his fault, and they did not talk about it on the train.

Camille excelled in the staircase scene—in which, after a naturally definitive quarrel, it was necessary to catch one another on the second step, with a clenched and tremulous hand.

In sum, she was an accomplished mistress:

Very young at thirty, of a reposed and cared-for beauty, ornamented with a genuinely aristocratic coquetry, without demi-mondaine equivocation.

It was, at any rate, on those indications alone that Jacques was able to build a series of hypotheses flattering for his self-esteem, for he knew nothing of Camille's life outside their rendezvous.

Interrogated by her friend, she became importunate, irritated, threatening not to come back again—and that threat immediately mastered the young lover, for whom the petty intrigue had rapidly become an omnipotent passion.

The thought of his mistress was mingled at present with all his occupations; the appearance of Camille floated like a fluid veil before his vision, modifying its aspects.

In that first contact with femininity, he found the key to an emotional life on the threshold of which he had previously wandered anxiously, without being able to penetrate it. Trouble before certain works of art to which he was subject, disturbed without comprehending, certain pieces of music of overwhelming charm, and the prestige of certain hours: all of that was explained by a single glance, a single inflection of the voice of the woman delivered in her languorous abandonment.

He recapitulated the adventure from the first encounter.

It was at a private viewing. In a little hall of engravings, a dazzling silhouette of spring fabrics in the midst of the gray of prints. An audacity pushing Jacques toward that woman, a quasi-involuntary compliment on the lips; his stupefaction, his near-chagrin on seeing himself greeted by a courtesan gaze. His even greater astonishment at the first steps of their intimacy, on discovering in his conquest a distinguished, cultivated, gracefully timorous woman evidently making her gallant debut.

Disinterested to the point of grimness, Camille was perfectly inexplicable, and the mystery that enveloped her became from day to day a torture more impossible to bear.

By degrees, Jacques' imagination was excited to the point of wanting to risk anything in order to penetrate that irritating unknown and take possession of the woman that fascinated him, to possess her in her future and in her revealed past, to unite their existence, since she alone represented, henceforth, the sole reason for living.

One evening, after a light meal that they had in Jacques' bedroom, a meal of lovers and birds in which they nibbled pastries and fruits without hunger, their hearts oppressed by the expectation of caresses, Jacques said:

"My darling Camille, I no longer want any mystery between us; I have the right not to want any, not only because I love you and you love me, but because I want to ask you to be my wife. Speak, my dear mistress; I've suffered so much from the shadow around you, and know, O beloved, that whatever the confessions might be to which you must resolve yourself, my resolution and my amour will not change."

"Jacques, I'm married," sighed Camille, pink with emotion.

"You'll get divorced."

"No."

"Since you love me, is your place not with me?"

"Don't interrogate me, my friend, and let's leave that subject. Content yourself with having in me a loving and agreeable mistress."

"I've obeyed you until now and haven't sought to know your secret, your life apart from me; speak now, extract me from trouble."

"Do you remember the fable of Amour and Psyche, and how dangerous it is to direct the investigative lamp at the object of your passion?"

Jacques conformed to the advice of the fable until the day when Camille's visits ceased abruptly.

Then, weaned from the joys the pleasant custom of which had plunged him into a sort of nirvana and ended up by putting to sleep even his curiosity about the woman, he put everything to work to pick up her trail.

And this is what he discovered.

The woman he loved, the wife of the rich old Baron X***, lived in the midst of a rapacious band of relatives lying in wait for the heritage promised to them if he died without children. The wife would then have been separated from that fortune with a modest share.

But the baronne did not want such a defeat. She resolved to give her husband a descendant.

By what succession of casuistical reasonings had she arrived at giving herself permission for a necessary adultery?

That is a problem that we shall leave to professional psychologists.

A year after the encounter of Jacques and Camille, the baron's son was baptized.

Camille, an honest woman, never saw her lover again, and did not even know that Jacques had left France in order to try to distract himself from his melancholy, repenting of having shed such a brutal light on the amiable penumbra that masked a banal adventure.

STONY GROUND
(*La Fronde*, 25 November 1898)

THE young Abbé du Plessys, since marquisette[1] has been holding him on the leash of a deceptive flirtation, is fading away visibly, scarcely able to sustain himself and only alimenting himself with candy and passion.

He escorts the inhumane woman along the pathways of the park, carrying her fan and her bouquet with a dying expression, as if that light weight were as heavy as that of a world.

As long as the gallant does not depart from the honest conversational tone in which the latest writings of Monsieur Diderot were discussed, an incident of gambling in the king's residence or the new painting by Greuse, marquisette puts the animation of a young cleric into matching him.

And it is necessary to see what it does to him, that animation!

Under the joyful frost of the powdered hair, the thin

---

1 Although this is obviously a proper name I have retained the author's affectation of only granting it a capital letter at the beginning of a sentence.

205

face becomes as pink as a Sèvres porcelain rose, and the large brown eyes shine like two amorous lamps.

But if the abbé ventures on to the terrain of declarations, marquisette lets him say all imaginable follies without getting annoyed—but with a gaze so distant, and such a visible expression of thinking about something else, that one would wager that she is no longer listening.

Marquisette adores animals—which sometimes causes Monsieur du Plessys to say, bitterly, that because of that, he conserves a little hope, meaning by that remark that love has rendered him as stupid as the most stupid of animals.

Marquisette has an aviary full of tame doves, which come in response to her voice with a delicate flutter to alight on her shoulders and her breast, thus forming a graceful garland worthy of the brush of Fragonard.

However, the preferred animal, the benjamin and the darling, is an undulating white lap-dog with a clownish face and a black nose: a rather roguish physiognomy.

One day, when marquisette is holding the dog in her arms, the abbé, sitting next to her, thoughtful and distracted, gives a kiss to the little favorite, which responds with a discourteous growl.

But marquisette, touched by the attention, returns Monsieur du Plessys' kiss, without quite knowing what she is doing.

THE STRANGE LIFE AND DEATH OF MONSIEUR LIEUE HOMAIN
(*La Fronde*, 25 November 1898)

THERE are singular destinies.

That of our friend Lieue Homain can be placed in that category without hesitation.

Born without opulence, he ruined himself by investing the brightest of his possessions in mortgages.

Then, once so adulated by his contemporaries, he was naturally showered with insults.

His character was embittered, and henceforth, he only nourished himself on hatred. That alimentation dilapidated him, as you can well imagine, and his stomach was in his heels.[1]

Thus, not at all well, he retired into himself, and was not known to have any other domicile thereafter.

He was, however, brave by nature.

His left hand did not know what his right hand was doing—which, to tell the truth, was not anything,

---

1 Although some of the colloquialisms with which this story is humorously crammed translate well enough into English, this one does not; its significance is, however, clear.

because of the hair that it comported. During rigorous winters, that hair in the hand constituted an economical means of heating for the young man.

In addition, he reduced all his expenses. The laundresses of his quarter could not earn anything from him, because he bleached himself by growing older.

Finally, having reached the age of forty-nine, he found a profession that was facile, if not very lucrative. He was going on fifty.

It was at that moment that he committed the most serious blunder of his life. Resolved to marry, he espoused a Quarrel. You can imagine what a Hell that was!

Our man, although full of strong qualities, could not support that blow with a serene soul. He lost his footing, and as his stomach was already in his heels, that disaggregated his organism considerably.

In the meantime, a few public events seemed to him to be so baroque that he threw up his arms.

"Everything passes," said a prophetic voice.

Shortly afterwards, he lost his head. The rest of him, seeing itself in such a piteous state, was devoured by shame.

IT'S RAINING . . .
(*La Fronde*, 10 December 1898)

IN the fiacre carrying her to the rendezvous, Geneviève becomes irritated—not by impatience, please God! She simply finds life absolutely dull and "quotidian," as the worthy Laforgue puts it. Her liaison, which is a year old, has already become almost as devoid of interest as the conjugal hearth after a decade.

Then the idea occurs to her of lodging in Vaugirard, although she lives in the Rue d'Amsterdam.

An obstinate rain is slapping the windows, suspended there in soft pearlettes, and the streets are framed there, black and confused, with the double gleam of gaslight reflected in puddles.

The lights add an ambient distress, rendering the fog more compact, and seem to pierce the damp sidewalks with fiery lances, building luminous subterranean colonnades and rendering the area vertiginous.

Here is the Place de la Concorde, a desert aggravated by the rumble of carriages that one cannot see.

Geneviève is not content.

A disagreeable little frisson climbs like a spider along her back. She wraps herself in her marten collar, calling herself stupid, and wonders in good faith why she is outside in this lousy weather.

On the bridge there is a new phantasmagoria of light: fiery palaces plunging into the Seine.

But all that is glacial, with the march of passers-by clawed by the wind, at war with mad umbrellas.

At that moment Geneviève remembers all her lover's little ridicules . . . And that black hairy birthmark near his moustache, decidedly unpleasant—by what mystery did she not notice that at the outset? That would have avoided many things. But bah! It's inelegant to take back what one has given—and then, there are things that one can't take back . . .

In any case, one can cross out.

The fiacre is rolling at present over the esplanade of Les Invalides, stuffed with fog and groaning in the north wind

Geneviève shrugs her shoulders with disdain on thinking about novelists who present adultery in rosy colors.

Finally, Geneviève and her fiacre reach the necropolitan quarter of Montmartre

Damn! A traffic jam. And in the obscurity, voices of pure absinthe are abusing one another.

Geneviève is ready to weep with anger, and does not know whether to carry on or go home.

Finally, the vehicle moves off again and jolts along the interminable Rue de Vaugirard.

The fog has dissipated slightly and the faces of pitiful greengrocers can be distinguished, with their displays of anemic carrots, decadent lettuces and stillborn apples.

The butcher's shops exhale their slaughterhouse odor, and in places, the electric dazzle of a large café plunges into a thicker obscurity the streets now swarming with a varied crowd.

"Where is the Passage des Favorites, then?"

It is the coachman who is questioning his client.

Geneviève is obliged to expose her plumed hat to the now-torrential downpour through the window in order to reply:

"You ought to know better than I do—it's your job. Ask a policeman. I don't even know where we are."

Her strength is at an end when they arrive at a genteel town house—the goal of the infernal journey.

As soon as the vestibule, while he takes her furs, a caress of discreetly perfumed warm air envelops her with wellbeing.

The veiled brightness of precious faiences retains the gaze and reposes it.

Geneviève's ill humor has already ceded to the charm of the familiar décor; a happy expansion relaxes her nerves. An atmosphere of intimacy completes her conquest.

They go into a dining room where the paintings of masters open windows into Dream in the wallpaper and the delicate odor floats of a refined meal, already served, without their being subjected to the inconvenience of domestics.

And as she passes before the large Venetian looking-glass Geneviève perceives her seductive silhouette beside that of her lover—she finds that they truly look good together—and she throws her arms around his neck, murmuring:

"Do you at least know that I love you extremely?"

He thanks the pretty lips that say such things with a kiss, and Geneviève returns his caress, all the way to the little black hairy birthmark, near to his moustache.

THE GOOD WOLVES
A Christmas Story
(*La Fronde*, 23 December 1898)

THAT day, old Cachyme rubbed her box-wood hands together as if she wanted to make sparks spring forth, so great was her joy at finally having vanquished the resistance of the beautiful Nadia, her niece.

Cachyme, the scorned, the ugly Cachyme, called a witch by the whole village, was about to have her proud revenge in giving her relative for a wife to Gregor, the king's own son.

Why, then, had she resisted for so long, that Nadia, all of whose soul quivered with tenderness toward the handsome prince who loved her?

Did she fear the haughty welcome of the ladies of the city, out there in the distant land to which her fear lord as about to take her? No, certainly not, for Gregor had caused all anxiety to vanish with words so persuasive that it would have been impossible not to believe him.

"Your beauty, my darling," he had assured her, "is so perfect that no princess possesses its like; you will therefore be more princess than all of them, by virtue of your charm."

Did her heart of a village girl bleed at leaving behind the humble companions of her young years: the wooly sheep that she took to the meadow, the pretty cow with the soft eyes, and the trees along the road, and the river that mirrored the sky? No, for with a single glance, Gregor had taught her to forget everything that was not his amour.

But there was a tragic secret in Nadia's life: she was a mother

In what violent and mysterious adventure her womb had conceived the wretched fruit, she did not know, the innocent, but the child, brought into the world a year ago, was of her blood and she cherished him like her soul.

Now, that terrible secret, Gregor could not know.

It would, therefore, be necessary to quit the poor mite forever.

And what would become of the child, whom no one would love?

Old Cachyme, who hated the infant mortally, had ended up putting Nadia's anxiety to sleep: "I'll take care of him, your little one, like the apple of my eye, and I'll love him more than my life; don't worry."

And Nadia, after having bathed her little boy with burning tears, who was also weeping, without under-standing, after thousands of kisses, left a heavy purse full of gold with old Cachyme and went with Gregor, her beloved, to the church, where an aged parish priest mar-ried them.

214

They were to depart the same evening; the horses hitched to the low sleigh were already whinnying.

But a sudden squall rendered the roads dangerous, so the aged priest sheltered the king's son and his bride until dawn the following day.

❋

Now, old Cachyme, ignorant of these things, said to herself: *Now that my niece is far away I'm going to get rid of that child. That way, I can keep all the gold for myself.* And she weighed the heavy purse in her hand complaisantly.

She therefore set forth, in spite of the squall, for the edge of the woods, carrying the little boy in her apron.

Having reached the side of the highway, as the cold was biting her legs, she placed the child on the ground and went back, without remorse, in spite of the menacing howls that were emerging from the forest.

The child, whom the monotonous stride of the old woman had rocked to sleep, woke up crying because of the cold. Terrible voices coming ever closer responded to his plaint, and two wolves found him, and sniffed the child, who started to smile at the approach of their warm breath and their gleaming eyes.

The midnight bells chimed at that moment the anniversary of the humble and glorious birth of a God, who had made himself poor and small. The holy voice of the bells floated in the icy air like a boat on the sea.

It was the blessed minute in which, once, the star of the Orient had guided the shepherds and the magi to the stable in which the one who commanded archangels lay, weak and naked, between the ox and the ass. Doubtless the young Jesus wrought a miracle and put tender pity into the hearts of the hungry wolves, for both of them lay down next to the abandoned child, protecting his body against the cold that would have killed him.

And the child, before going to sleep, surrounded the neck of one of them with an affectionate arm, while the other licked his face, on which his last tears were freezing.

✳

The next day, the princely sleigh followed the same road; the king's son was taking his beautiful wife to his court.

The road to travel was long, but the delight of the united couple was so great that the trees seemed to be running ahead and saluting them respectfully.

Nadia, although she was very happy, was stifling sighs in thinking about her child, when the two wolves, lying on the ground like good domestic dogs, attracted the attention of the newlyweds.

The prince, astonished, had the horses stop and got down, followed by his wife, in order to see the strange group at closer range.

"Ah! Madame, my darling, will we have less compassion than those two beasts?" he cried, on perceiving the sleeping child.

And he held him out to Nadia, who received him in her arms, swooning with emotion, wonderstruck and joyful to the point of taking away her intelligence.

"Keep him, Madame," said the prince, "and serve as his mother, for such is doubtless the Divine Will."

"My dear Lord," she replied, in tears, and putting one knee on the ground, while she pressed her child to her delighted heart with a tremulous arm, "you are as good as the angels in Heaven, and you have made me the happiest of women."

THE CHRONICLE OF THE KINGS
(*La Fronde*, 7 January 1899)

THE famous wisdom of nations, accustomed to so many blunders, is nevertheless sometimes right.

Thus, the unanimous tradition of placing at the beginning of the year symbolic legends of hope, is ingenious and generous.

Long before the approach of the sad season of old age, we know lassitude, discouragement and the bitterness of the effort that struggles against a hostile atmosphere, the dolorous collapse of illusions, and inevitable disenchantment.

Then, what recrudescence of melancholy comes to us with every stroke of the implacable chime of the clock of time: one year more. And what dejection overwhelms us before the necessity of perpetual recommencements.

It is at the first, chagrined step that we find the comforting Christian legends: a Child born for the advent of fraternity and charity.

The kings of the Orient travel through deserts and forests, their hands filled with precious gifts.

A star accompanies them. And the fatigue of the road is forgotten in the haste to see the great King—very small—born in Bethlehem.

A star guides them—and the darkness is dissipated, the night becomes like the most beautiful day.

For that star is Hope.

It shines at the highest point of the sky with an incomparable light, and if our tearful eyes contemplate it, our very tears will become pure jewels, networks of gold spun in its clarity.

At familial tables the *gâteau des rois* brings young and old together. Petty rancors are reconciled and appeased; a mist of benevolence floats above the white sheet.

An innocent malice makes the bean fall to the tall timid fellow who loves his cousin without daring to tell her so.

However, he needs a queen.

It is done—no one knows how.

And here are their naïve majesties, chatting together and laughing, at last.

The king drinks . . .

However, the season is rude.

A sky heavy with snow and rain.

An angry wind capsizes the leafless branches. It seems that all the flowers are dead forever . . . that the cheerful sun will never be seen again, nor the green expanses.

But after a maddening course through Paris over the slippery pavement, after conflicts with the coachmen of fiacres full of arrogance and adulterated wine, one returns home.

And immediately, a delightful bouquet—a present left by a friend—makes you forget all annoying misadventures.

Those tea-roses are so touching—a pious lie of hot-houses—and those mimosas come from far away.

How their hearts of gold contain all the lost sunshine and the hope of radiant seasons!

How their pale perfume, which exalts the flame of the coke in the fireplace, speaks of the return of suave breezes!

And what a consoling thing is amity!

It is also the week in which the very small are kings.

For them, the shops have become palaces of enchantment. Polichinelle is surpassed.

The little girls hugging in their arms dolls whose enamel eyes are alarmed are already initiated into the frisson of future maternities, and the little boys on mechanical horses are training for later parades.

The diversity of toys—violins, paint-boxes, books of travels, marital harness—already solicits the childish hand in a significant fashion; vocations are revealed.

And while still insouciant, the little beings savor the possession of those marvels, the secret desire or which is perceived by a vigilant heart, a star lights up on high: the star of their destiny.

They will follow it, later, through deserts and hostile path; they will follow it intrepidly, mastering their lassitude, their eyes fixed on its prestigious light, as were those of the royal Magi long ago.

OTHERS
(*La Fronde*, 10 February 1899)

EVEN now, after six years of rupture, certain objects glimpsed in an identical light, certain streets once walked together, certain sorrows of the weather, and memorials, strike her with the mortal blow that makes her relive, as if in true agonies, all of their past life in a single minute.

A dolorously exquisite epoch, that year of anxious, combative and absorbing happiness.

The combination had been strange of the lover he was, that delicately nervous fellow of debilitated but stubborn will, new to amour, not knowing how to abandon himself to it, and her, the despotic mistress delivered entirely, with the constant exaltation that does not suffer mediocrity in the adversary. For are not two genuinely passionate lovers adversaries?

So, from that year of quasi-common life, did there remain to both of them a bitter aftertaste of battles, as if some rude hurricane of an angry sea had shaken their hearts, leaving on their disunited lips a subtle and tenacious salt?

The last chapter of that brief romance was singular and piteous.

Everything was decided that night, precisely when two beings sensed that they were on the redoubtable edge of the Absolute, in embraces that were like glorious death.

And the mistress spoke thus, her hair spread out over the pillow like wings ready to take flight, her two arms linked around her lover's head:

"My friend, my very dear friend, we are attaining at this moment the very gates of the Garden promised to humans worthy of seeing it face to face.

"This is not the light and gallant Paradise into which Watteau leads his pretty powdered ladies to play at amour and blind man's buff; no, the Happiness that we are attaining is a grave and formidable thing.

"We have picked all the delicate flowers of tenderness and we have perfumed our lips with them, but it is only presently that the Gate, the great Gate of the sumptuous Dream, the Gate that opens so rarely, will unclose its battens for us with the sound of the sea breaking on the rocks.

"Are you not afraid, my beloved?

"It would be derisory and frightful to survive the joy in which we shall bathe, as if in an ocean inflamed by the dying sun, and we shall die ourselves, I tell you, O my very dear friend, after having savored that hour. For myself, I am ready and palpitating with courage, but if you are afraid, my friend, flee me!"

"Madness, madness!" he replied, having become pale, mordant and distraught, his curls crazy.

But Fear entered into his faint heart.

And he fled in the morning, far, far away; compressing, beneath his two hands, the black blood escaping from the wound that he had made in his faint heart by tearing himself away from that amour.

Now, the years had made their indifferent water flow over those forgotten dolors.

Now, one evening, *She* passed, in a street once walked together, in the bleak gaslight, the silhouette of a man stopped, immobilized stiffly, as if dead of emotion . . .

It was *Him* . . .

She could not see his face, but no doubt was possible.

She knew too well the elegant surge of that body, in which she alone had given birth to powerful and profound sensualities.

She took flight without knowing why she was fleeing, but he had also recognized her. He soon caught up with her, bewildered, and took possession of her tremulous arm.

And already, before daring to plunge one gaze into another, all the poorly-died amour was resuscitated and clamored, demanding its prey of kisses, bites and ancient embraces.

The street was dark but, without even seeing his companion, he said:

"O my love, my unique love! I shall realize, then, the Dream that once made my faint heart totter: dying in an excessively formidable Happiness.

"Perhaps you are cured of our tenderness, but no matter, you cannot refuse me the charity of being the ideal and funereal Portal. Come!"

Oh, no, she was not cured, and that dear voice—his voice!—how it awoke the emotions of old, living and burning as on the first day!

By what divine hazard did they find themselves before his house?

He carried her off like a prey, to the bed, widowed of its beauty for six years, and their embrace, sobbing, dolorous and joyful, exhausted them, left them devoid of strength and thought, during unforgettable hours savored like a spiritual opium . . .

In the depths, however, in the utmost depths of both their souls, the bitter waves of a rising melancholy unfurled.

Those years, those cruel years, how had *the other* lived them?

In what arms had *he* sought forgetfulness?

On what heart had *she* slept?

She spoke first.

"I want to see your face again, O my beloved, and kiss your eyes and lips, your dear eyes, the haunting of which has never quit me."

Summoned by a bell, a domestic as silent as a phantom brought lighted lamps.

O vertigo and stupor!

It was not *him*, and nor was it *her!*

But the embrace that held them united did not break its bond.

For he was like a him even more resembling, a new him, scarcely different, but how much more the man she had always wanted, whom he had never been completely.

And it was her too, almost, but more beautiful and with, more than the other, all the intellectual charm that he had sought in vain in the arms of the lost mistress.

O enchantment! It was not the resurrection of the dead, the old Amour, but a glorious nativity of Amour, made of forgetfulness and the pardon of pains suffered,

And on that night, only, was the wish granted that the lovers had formed far apart from one another, in other beds, where they had been waiting for one another without knowing it.

The Gate—the great Gate of sumptuous Dream that unclosed so rarely—opened its battens for them with the sound of the sea breaking on the rocks.

And the pale dawn found them both dead, linked by an invincible embrace.

A RIDICULOUS GAMBLER
(*La Fronde*, 24 March 1899)

"WHAT you have just related there, my dear, brings me back, by a bizarre and mysterious path, to a memory. It relates to the epoch of my life when, gripped by the passion and habit of gambling, I was curled up in the bosom of a signal brutalization."

"What a charming pillow!"

"Yes, I had, at that moment, the exact effect of a dead man galvanized solely by the contact of the diabolical cards and the cabalistic vocables of baccarat.

"*Banco à cheval* appeared to me to be a phrase far more eloquent than the famous *Let him die*.

"A 'hand' was not at all what a Phidias or a Praxiteles might believe, who would not have failed to define the object in question, falsely, as follows: a hand is a part of the human body, infinitely expressive, worthy of all the care of an artist who ought to make it speak, in the beautiful plastic language, of the race if the being to whom it belongs and his life; his strength or his grace, his nature as a god—or goddess—a hero or a boor.

"No, a 'hand' was several samples of fifty-two cards shuffled and cut; and that same hand could be admirable or noxious, according to whether it was you or another who won by its means.

"The sole benefit that I obtained from that inadmissible series of months dilapidated in the monomania of gaming—which, by excess, maltreated me more generally—is, perhaps, having been able to penetrate a little into the psychology of the gambler. It is even one of the rare ones that one can undertake in good faith, for, under the lash of that particular neurosis, a kind of doubling of the individual is produced. While one side of the self, delirious with superstitious nonsense, absurd hopes, black and unjustifiable discouragements, speaks the banalities that ought to figure in a self-respecting 'party,' the other side of the same self observes and disapproves, is not proud of belonging to such an uninteresting whole, plunged into a state so close to imbecility.

"Outside the battlefield, stormier than the angry sea, that the green baize is, the psychic state of the gambler is curious and lamentable. He wanders, prey to an immense ennui, adrift, his nerves having become receptive and sensitive, like musical instruments susceptible to crises of hilarity, ever ready for tears, ceding to a distress without object but not without mildness.

"That state is favorable to all sensational transpositions. All aberrations are possible and create an artificial life as intense as real life, and more so.

"It was, therefore in those dispositions that I was in bed, the curtain hermetically closed, on a day already in decline, after having returned home at dawn.

"From the courtyard a voice came, of dream, a seraphic voice, a child's voice, a voice of a soul.

"Nothing was as crystalline, as transparent, as young, as that timbre, and yet abysms of melancholy and avalanches of pathos vibrated therein; it was like a synthesis, like a triple extract, if I dare say so, of all that can make pity shudder and compassion pant. It was the very echo of universal dolor.

"It was as sad as a river formed of tears, on which little boats of mourning are descending with the current, charged with our dearest memories, plaintive phantoms.

"The little silver hammer of that voice seemed to strike our heart, become sonorous crystal, exactly at the secret corners where a remorse or a regret sleeps.

"Harmonies full of sweet and distressing notes, fluid cascades, emotional surfaces.

"What could the words of that song be? In what language of what country, in what dialect, were they proffered?

"Distance allowed a blissful uncertainty to float over it, and no speech could be worth as much as the prestige of that mystery.

"From what singular being did that voice emanate?

"A woman, doubtless, who seemed the youngest of the angels.

"But most probably, it was the voice of a child as yet unconscious of her beauty, the voice of a little girl with the throat of a nightingale. A blonde voice.

"She expanded that voice at moments like a sidereal clarity, a complete firmament of ecstasy, and drew us among the orbs of starts rotating in unlimited space.

"It penetrated like a dazzling light into the most obscure and dustiest corridors of the soul, dislodging the egotistical and base sentiments, which died with a shameful flutter of wings, like bats surprised by the sun. An emollient repentance oiled the traces left by customary annoyances.

"What poverty, all that time lost in paltry vicious practices! That mania for gambling, for instance!—thus I monologued—oh, to live henceforth as irreproachable as the chevalier Bayard, at least. To take one's joy in the joy that expends around one . . . ! And how much more judicious wisdom that would be, even a better calculation—how much cleverer, in sum.

"I dissolved in sanctity, I was edifying, mystical, melancholy and radiant.

"That voice made of me what it wanted.

"And as the warmth of the bed gradually sent me back to sleep and finished cretinizing my understanding, I committed this fault:

"'Oh, if such a voice took me by the hand, I would climb to the most albescent summits.'

"However, the voice shut up and I found the courage to leap barefoot on to the carpet and run to the window with some money wrapped in paper.

"I was just in time; my chanteuse was going away.

"It was a poor old woman in ruins, a decrepitude scarcely alive, folded and heaped toward the death the color of which she bore in her face, ravaged by cracks and wrinkles.

"At the same moment my concierge bought me my letters, which he accompanied with this commentary on seeing me in contemplation before the consternating cantatrice:

"'She hasn't too bad a voice at her age, especially when one thinks that she drinks every day . . . she is, thank God, well enough known for that in the quarter.'"

APRIL CHRONICLE
(*La Fronde*, 14 April 1899)

AFTER the knells, already distant, of the penitential week, the Easter bells have expired in the April air, and here comes the odorous carillon of woodland lilies of the valley and all the hasty corollas of fruit trees.

In spite of the dramas, in spite of the hatreds, in spite of the dryness of hearts, this suave moment of the year is a truce.

On the edge of eyelids that the first sunlight causes to blink, something trembles that resembles an affectionate tear.

That, you see, is because the chestnut trees of Parisian promenades do not read the newspapers, and the violets are not up to date.

So, rising from their vegetal womb with the first breath of spring is an odor of the Golden Age, of candid effluvia to which the best of us cling. The simple *we*, the animal *we*, the *we* that is brother to the sparrows and the squirrels, the mild calves and the good pigs.

And the question arises: why is there so much interiority in the human animal, compared to other animals?

Have you ever seen a dog rendered ridiculous by vanity, boring his canine colleagues with a eulogy of his merits?

Has a horse jealous of the success of a competitor on the track ever tripped him up to make him fall?

On the contrary; if the dog barks recklessly it is because he has heard the groan of some poor devil of another dog, locked up or chained up in some distant place.

I have been told the story of a cat that maintained relations of amity with a rabbit, tainted with an air of protection if you wish, but how faithful in misfortune!

When the unfortunate rabbit had suffered the unjust and revolting fate to which rabbits are assigned, which is to finish at the bottom of a stewpot—*de profundis*—the good cat, which had protested in vain by means of heart-rending mewling, took possession of the remains, of the poor skin of his comrade, and carried it away to the place where it had the habitude of sitting, and watched over that relic, which he covered with caresses; and it would have been perfectly dangerous to attempt to steal it from him, for his melancholy then turned to the greatest anger.

And yet, the human animal has a hundred times as many motives as the others for sensing a solidarity and a fraternity with his peers.

Whereas the children of animals come into the world fully clad—in a princely fashion, if you please—capable after a few days getting out of trouble and defending themselves, the human child, debilitated and stupid for several years—there are even some who continue in the same vein until the end—expects protection care and maintenance from all his fellows, and only owes his life to their devotion. However, having reached the age of strength, armed for defense, he immediately thinks of attack, and rejoices more in the defeat of the other than in his own success.

Has a royal tiger poisoner ever been seen?

Has there been since the earth has been habited by living beings, a wild beast, a reptile or a raptor ingenious enough to torment and to persecute, to refine mental and physical tortures as humans have done in all times: massacring, gehennaing, burning and burying their fellows alive?

Filthy beasts!

We declare, with the pride particular to our race, that animals are inferior to us in intelligence because they do not manifest it externally in accordance with our mode of judgment.

But perhaps it is our judgment that is limited and their disdain is manifest by works, an attitude of pride, and a contemplative state far superior to our agitations.

I am not far distant from defining our species thus: "Human, an inferior animal in which it pleases God to manifest himself occasionally, which then become a great Artist."

But we have strayed a long way from the cheerful and innocent suggestions of the Easter fortnight, which is the matter in hand.

That period, with its trees in flower—if one distances oneself slightly from Paris—appears like a white bouquet, a bridal bouquet.

And are there not, every year—in spite of the bloody seed of Cain—untiring espousals of Nature, who has had the weakness of retaining her ovaries, with Spring?

He returns, that Spring, ever young, with a sprig of lilac in his buttonhole, mounted on a bright spirited charger whose hooves ring on the reflowered roads.

He returns, the Spring, handsome, gallant and chivalrous—not knowing that all of that has become unfashionable.

THE KID
(*La Fronde*, 28 April 1899)

"What are you called, my little friend?"

"Maurice," sobbed the kid.

"Well, Maurice, it's necessary not to cry any longer; children who cry are very tedious, and you'll make your face dirty. How old are you?"

"Six."

She is a pretty, elegant lady, like the ladies in images, who admonishes the poor kid dressed in mourning.

Maurice has just lost his mother—the father had preceded her by a year, so Maurice is now alone in the world.

That isn't cheerful.

And to increase the pain it will be necessary to quit the pleasant village where he was born, the farmyard where he played so much with Tom, the big dog, and, finally, Tom himself.

The lady is taking him to Paris.

Madame de Breuilly, who has been his cousin, strictly speaking, all his life, because of a misalliance—which is to say, a poor marriage—is humanizing herself for the sake of the orphan and taking responsibility for him. It isn't the boy's fault, is it?

And then, it will be very decorative to be the benefactress of her family.

He is lucky, the child.

The child, however, while she is giving her final orders for the departure to the domestic, has escaped into the garden to say goodbye to all the fine trees, comrades of his childhood, and the vegetable garden bordered by redcurrant bushes, and to weep loudly—so loudly that Tom has come running and the most heart-rending of adieux recommences amid the child's sobs and the plaintive growls of the animal.

Installed in Paris, Maurice continues to give the impression of doubting his good fortune.

It is the period of the Easter vacation, and while waiting to go to school he wanders through the luxurious apartment, with nothing to do—*soulless*, as they say in his village.

His new residence is, however, charming in its modern luxury.

The drawing room is lacquered in bright green, the fragile chairs and sofas upholstered with magical silks embroidered with exotic flowers and birds.

Japanese screens with sumptuous gold and silver monsters.

In the dining room, stained-glass descends all the way to the floor with a narrow window in delightful tones, framed with large opaline and topaz cabochons. The support is in square cabochons the color of water running under trees—green water.

Madame de Breuilly has very little time to devote to her protégé, so he profits from that to lead the existence of a dreamy poet.

That stained-glass is one of his stations of predilection. While the sunlight is broken up by its sharp ridges, Maurice sees again the matinal awakening in the branches, and the delicate pink skies of evening in the roseate central pane.

Another elevated sympathy is for the bronze wolf, signed Barye,[1] on the mantelpiece.

With a similar shade, one could swear that it was Tom, and Maurice's affectionate heart is induced to a gaffe of which he is not proud.

One day he approached the bronze work of art tenderly with a sugar lump in his fingers, which he put under the nose of the fake pooch.

As you can imagine, it was a flop, and Maurice was vexed.

Deep down, since he has entered into the rich and luxurious dwelling, Maurice has amused himself, above all, in being mortally bored.

Sometimes, Madame de Breuilly takes him out in her carriage, but the din of the Parisian streets terrifies him,

1 The Romantic sculptor Antoine-Louis Barye (1795-1875) was particularly noted for his sculptures of animals.

spoiling the pleasure that he might obtain from that new spectacle

He remembers delightedly a halt at the Louvre museum, Madame de Breuilly having arranged a rendezvous with another lady in the Galerie Française.

Maurice, refined by precocious misfortune, is able to savor in his naïve fashion the evocative art of beautiful landscapes, rediscovering cherished memories therein. While passing through the other halls he came to a stop before van Ostade's pigs:[1] the blissful piglets amid the gilded straw of the sty, gilded themselves with good sunlight.

So, a few weeks later, when Madame de Breuilly said to him: "Go and get dressed, Maurice, we're going to the Louvre," he clapped his hands with joy.

This time, however, it was to the Louvre department store that they were going, to be trampled and jostled. His disappointment was great.

Finally, the hour for school sounded.

Maurice felt neither pain nor pleasure at that, merely a little fear, and he thought, with a tender regret, about the alphabet that Monsieur le Curé had shown him in the pleasant lessons taken with a few comrades in the dining room illuminated by a small window green with branches, scented by ripe pears.

---

1 The reference is to a 1644 painting by Isaac Jans van Ostade, not the slightly earlier and better-known painting of pig-slaughterers by Adriaen van Ostade.

His reverie was so profound, and rendered him so bewildered at the moment of penetrating into the classroom, that his future schoolfellows, in spite of the severe eye of the junior master, could not help exclaiming, while laughing:

"Oh, that head!"

"That face!"

"That mug!"

MAY
(*La Fronde*, 12 May 1899)

OF the months of May, the May of old, I have only retained tenuous memories. The archangelic ceremonies of the evening, services of the Virgin fêted among immaculate flowers and the seraphic responses of the choir were too imponderable, too intangible, too su-praterrestrial, and could not leave a greater imprint than a pretty dream.

What I remember forcefully are certain Sunday afternoons in the country church attached to the convent.

This happened in Galician Poland in the year . . . you don't need to know.

The nuns were standing in the choir, and through the grille one could see their white and black cornets fluttering like great caged birds.

We pupils, in our secular quality, were crammed into the first benches under the vigilant spying eyes of saintly little girls.

In the nave, there was a crowd of peasants of both sexes seated in piety and meditation, the men standing near the door, the wives and young women kneeling closer to the main altar, in the gaiety of their chemises embroidered with colored wool and their scarlet and blue skirts.

The light of the stained-glass windows melted all those tones, and tinted the heavy blonde tresses with violet and crimson.

The batten of the door opened sometimes, to fall back heavily on a latecomer; then a white light as fresh as a moist candle or a small waterfall filtered under the apse, bringing a perfume of new grass, young leaves and beasts in the pasture.

But after a certain time, the door no longer slammed, and the divine service was celebrated in the silence of the crowd, only interrupted from time to time by a sigh provoked by the devotion mingled with the lack of air, easily sensible for throats habituated to respiring in the limitless plain. After the mass, a large party of the men quit the place in order to go, henceforth in regulation with their spiritual duties, to cultivate the spirituous, at the tavern, by drinking grain alcohol.

Then a voice in the choir gave the signal for the canticle to the Virgin:

"*A-ve Mari-a . . .*"

And it seemed that to all those women, united to praise her, Mary herself said: "Finally, here we are, just between us . . ."

All the young village girls intoned the canticle in a rich unison in which the different timbres constituted a subtle and warm symphony, produced like an orchestral effect.

The ardent brunettes were the vibrant cellos of the low notes. Those who still retained in their tresses the gold of early age provided the limpid sound of flutes, like an Arcadian suggestion. Poignant altos sang among those whose hearts had known the laceration of mourning and abandonments.

And all those exaltations, those candors and those intimate emotions united in order to form a kind of melodic river flowing placidly in broad expanses.

It was an old canticle in Gregorian plainsong, of a simple and beautiful character. *Ave* burst forth on a triumphantly high, laudatory note, which descended for *Maria* to a passionate and humiliating medium, associating the epic of the Dolorous Mother with human miseries.

The light of the stained-glass windows projected violent floods of orange, azure or emerald, sometimes over the altar-cloth, on which it seemed to sow armfuls of flowers, and sometimes among the pillars, where it put a flock of magical peacocks, in order momentarily to embrace the choir where the nuns were standing, as if in an apotheosis.

And I thought that the old religious air was once sung in warrior camps when Christianity was battling the Turk, the Cross against the Crescent.

And that became admirable, those rude, almost savage heroes attributing their bloody victories to the protection of the celestial Virgin, for whom the Slav peoples have a particular devotion. They saw her marching at the head of their dogged cohorts, the Minerva of a new cult, and they went to death and glory confident in Her and in the sanctity of their cause, which was to deliver oppressed brethren from the Muslim yoke.

That was the epoch of barbarity.

Time has moved on, and civilization too. Indifference and egotism have replaced generous impulses, the desire for noble actions . . .

JEANNE
(*La Fronde*, 26 May 1899)

YOUNG Jeanne who only arrived in Paris a week ago, already regarded the great city as an inferno of bewilderment, misery and humiliation.

Expelled from the natal house—she was from Nanteuil—by her stepmother following the death of her father, she had descended at the Gare de l'Est with fifty francs that her poor father had slipped into her hand surreptitiously on his death-bed.

She would obtain a situation in Paris as a maidservant, she thought, and she had already deposited her fifty francs with an employment agent indicated to her by a policeman, with a deep sigh of regret. At present she spent her days in the nauseating stink of a host of paupers waiting like her.

Harassed by time and hunger, she went in search of some infimal eatery, emerging every time more terrified in seeing her petty treasure melt away, reducing her meals progressively. When the bureau closed in the evening, she went back to her rat-hole in a furnished-hotel-and-wine-shop of criminal appearance, where the noise of arguments and brawls kept her awake far into the night.

Poor little Jeanne, fifteen years of age, had the candid youth and delicate beauty of her patron saint, the heroine of Orléans, but not the warrior soul and the bravery.

She had, on the contrary, a poor pusillanimous and cowardly soul, frightened by everything.

So she spent her nights weeping, with loud sobs of fear, before the menacing life that was opening before her, full of suffering, disappointments, privations and dangers.

One day, the agent finally gave her an address, and the same day, the delighted Jeanne, believing that all her troubles were at an end, took her little valise to the home of Monsieur and Madame Ogret, drapers established in the Boulevard de la Chapelle.

Madame, a very fat lady, gave the impression of an elephant to whom the good God might have been given without confession; Monsieur, short and fat, rolled bloodshot eyes and shouted at everyone, but fundamentally, would not have hurt a fly.

With the consequence that, when Jeanne went back to her own little bed in the attic after a hard day, she felt completely tranquil and happy.

Her labor, although hard, pleased her. After crude work in the kitchen, there was making up the bedrooms to do. Wiping the stupid trinkets that garnished the shelves, applying a feather duster to the bad taste displayed everywhere, gave her a sensation of acquired wealth.

That lasted for several months when, at the beginning of April, Monsieur became bizarre with her. The scolding voice, in speaking to her—how can I put it?—became tender. And I beg you to believe that it was terrible.

Now that May is about to end, all the events pass through the passive and vanquished mind of the young woman again, as a hideous nightmare.

She sees the old man coming into her room one night, without shoes, snuffling like an invalid.

Before the terror of the child, which was about to be translated in screams:

"You'll wake the boss lady . . . and she'll throw you out."

And she was even more afraid of being thrown out.

A month later:

"You're going to pack your bag, my girl, and get out this very day."

It is Madame who is speaking.

"But what have I done, Madame?" weeps the little maidservant.

"You're a brazen hussy to ask me that. She can no longer fit into her skirts."

Loquaciously, Madame continues to preach on the subject of the profligacy of servants.

"So young, with her innocent air, who would believe it!"

And then on the respectability of the house, and on this and that; a curiosity to confess the child, to know the guilty party, almost makes her soften.

"I'd like to keep you, my poor girl, but I can't; there'd be a scandal."

And it is thus that Jeanne learns that she is pregnant and is thrown into the street, by that little rascal Spring.

FOR MADELON
(*La Fronde*, 26 May 1899)

THE humble funeral procession follows the road bordered with poplars.

Preceded by a priest in a surplice and the choirboy whose clogs sound on the stones, the bier is carried by four peasants.

Behind the coffin covered in black cloth with a white cross, which lurches to the rhythm of the march, a haggard old woman follows, staggering, as if drunk.

It is her son that is being carried away under the black cloth, her handsome François, who had no peer for work in the fields, and also for songs in the evening.

And then, another day, in the tavern, for that accursed Madelon with her fortune-teller eyes, two young men had picked a quarrel, and then bottles and tankards had been thrown at the height of the brawl. Before anyone could intervene, François, her François, fell with a fractured skull.

He had fallen, the robust fellow, with a bloody shred of his rival's flesh between his teeth and the name of the girl. He fell like a bellicose stag in the amorous season.

And now it is smiling everywhere, the ingenuous spring season, unconscious of its misdeeds. The young leaves are quivering and stirring in the sunlight with a delicate sound, as if beaten by a rain of light. The azure is transparent and the grass constellated by corollas.

The weeping woman sees that freshness and those splendors, torn apart by the prism of her tears. The sunlight is frayed there like a golden rag, the suave colors of the calices in the grass dissolving into an infinitely gray melancholy mud.

For he is there, in that box, motionless forever, the agile youth, her happiness and her pride. The old mother, haggard, as if drunk, follows the procession, tottering.

Memories return to her quasi-demented brain, memories of the time when the gamin drank from her tears with the gazes of Paradise, exactly like those of the angels on the main altar of the church.

Now they are approaching that church, and the mother's heart breaks with grief, while in the little cemetery, as green and flowery as a bouquet, a multitude of birds, joyful and tender, sing the triumphant spring, the irresponsible spring, amid the fervent scents of resins and saps.

IN THE GRASS
(*La Fronde*, 23 June 1899)

To Anna Bruère

OH, the delightful landscape!

Let's sit down, my dear, in this long grass, and, without talking about anything any longer, let's deliver ourselves, as if to a calm current, to the effluvia, to these sounds to the beauty of this décor.

At our feet, at the bottom of the bank, there is the sparkling, shiny Marne, green, silver and blue, receiving in its bosom the staging of the hills and the traveling clouds, striped by the slow glide of yawls.

Opposite, on the edge of the woods, with sentinel poplars, and, around us, hiding everything if we wished, the undulating forest of crazy oats.

It seems that those oats surpass in height the nearby treetops when we lie down under their light plumes, and put blonde veils over our cheeks and eyes.

A turtle-dove is lamenting in the wood, a sly blackbird mocks its trouble.

That reminds me of the story you kindly told me about the young girl who . . .

But enough stories, no matter how well told they might be.

Let us respire in silence the fresh odor of the earth, the balms exhaled by the wild mint and the flowering elder.

It is the month when the pollens snow. Can you see them fluttering like a swarm? The petals of acacias pass in a perfumed squall.

What do I see? Ramoneau, the good dog, is bringing us the newspapers!

Go away, Ramoneau, we don't want to know anything.

WOODLAND PATH
(*La Fronde*, 23 June 1899)

LISE, in a pink shirt, and Pierre, her promise, follow the mauve path through the hornbeam wood, which makes a décor of laughing youth and blonde languor for their youth and their languor.

Above, the branches extend a green awning into which the breeze puts delicate eddies; the shadows of the leaves beat wings then and flutter like butterflies.

On the ground, beneath the thickness of the woods, a river of milk is spread, under a filtration of light that shiny mirrors of ivy reflect, amid the fresh fans of strawberry bushes.

The thin trunks seem to be spinning in a round-dance of svelte hamadryads, delivered to their games.

But Pierre and Lise do not see anything of all that, nor the whips of the long grass that borders the path, describing elegant spirals in falling back, which the sunlight transforms to gold ornaments: ewers with casual handles, silver scrolls and garlands.

Oh! Our lovers are no longer visible. Where the devil have they gone?

Only the mingled voices of birds animate the luminous solitude.

The chaffinch weaves his trills, the magpie repeats a slow ,phrase obstinately, and the sparrow chirps, put in a good mood by the morning full of balms and light.

At intervals, the entire chattering society falls silent, as if to listen in the depths of the forest to the quivering of leaves and branches, like the sound of a distant waterfall.

✳

Lise and Pierre come back, tenderly enlaced.

Well! It's high time!

The sun has descended completely to the horizon and fills in the voids left by the entanglement of foliage with diamonds, topazes, rubies and incandescent gold.

A sumptuous pyre seems to have been ignited behind the trees, where all the treasures of Golconda and Colorado are burning.

The light spread out there is like a joyous flame reflected in the facets of the vegetation.

But at present the lovers see the marvels that surround them, and understand the dialect of the birds.

The Child with soft gazes hidden under a blindfold, Amour, the initiator of all splendor, has opened their eyes and revealed Beauty.

THE VIRGIN OF THE LAMBS
(*La Fronde*, 23 June 1899)

A delightful tableau!

Madame Paul is sitting in the courtyard of her house, with a little boy two years old playing in the sand at her feet and another, not yet weaned, on her knees.

But it is not her child that the peasant woman is feeding at the moment; it is a young white lamb that is drinking greedily from the bottle that she is extending to it; another white lamb, which appears to be the same one, reflected in a mirror, is bleating impatiently, waiting its turn.

The younger of the children sinks his little hand into the wool of the patient lamb, dazzling wool reminiscent of milk, snow and pearls.

Where are you, Masters, Fra Angelico of the naïve palette and precious Memling, to fix that gracious image, to make a *Holy Family* or an *Agnus Dei*, some pious painting impregnated with mildness, faith and pity extended even to innocent fraternal animals

Aren't they dainty, those lambs? There is no means of confusing them with papas and mamans, sheep and ewes; they are true babies with pert faces, gay and gauche movements full of the charm of infancy.

I draw nearer; the brilliant immaculate fleeces attract me magnetically; I would like to kiss those genteel cheeks, fleeing a trifle fearfully.

"They're truly exquisite, your nurslings, Madame Paul."

"Yes," she replies to me with a hint of pride, in the same way that she accepts compliments on her own progeniture. "Yes, they're nice. When they've been killed they'll make a nice rug for my brats."

THE LEGACY
(*La Fronde*, 28 July 1899)

MADEMOISELLE CUNÉGONDE DE BRANY had asked her sister to leave her daughter Lucile with her for a month when she left the convent where the child was concluding her studies.

It would be a little youth, a little gaiety in her enclosed, quasi-religious life. She had only quit the cloister after the dispersal of her order in 18**, but she remained a nun of sorts in her laic life and did not quit her little province, never going out except to church, where she spent the greater part of her days.

She dressed in black, with improbable hats, ugly by design, only receiving priests, who were accused in low voices of cultivating her in the hope of a pious legacy from her considerable fortune.

Some, better informed, claimed that the holy men were wasting their time, Aunt Cunégonde having left everything to her niece.

Lucile's mother granted her sister's request all the more gladly because she was counting on the grace and gentility of Lucile to complete the conquest of that aunt, who was not negligible.

One day, therefore, Lucile disembarked in the austere dwelling of Mademoiselle de Brany.

She was youth personified, little Lucile. Blonde and curly-haired, like an angel—the eyes, of course, were more diabolical: dark green, almost black, with long silky lashes. The face was all pink and white, like a pretty ornament in Saxe porcelain, and a figure that one feared seeing break, so slender was it.

Aunt Cunégonde did not take long to discover, with amazement, that the gamine was fifteen years old—which ought to have been measurable in the forty-eight centimeters of her waist, tightened mortally in order to lose two or three more, the opinion of demoiselles being that, at that game above all, whoever loses wins.

But the good aunt was destined to have many other surprises with Mademoiselle Lucile.

In the meantime, she savored the truly exquisite feast of all that adolescence in bloom. The voice was like the twittering of a warbler, the smile made one think of milk spilled into a rose, to be drunk by some greedy sylph, and the diabolical eyes nevertheless had the limpidity of lively springs reflecting soft shade.

But what discomfitures from the moral point of view!

When Mademoiselle de Brany took her niece to church, it was in vain that, during the most moving parts of the sermon, she searched for pious emotions in Lucile's face; the mademoiselle amused herself suffering martyrdom in shoes that were too small, even though her feet were already naturally imperceptible.

"Let's take a look at your cheeks," said Aunt Cunégonde, anxiously, one day. "Do you have a fever? They have a violet tint."

Under the inspecting finger, however, the girl retained the velvet freshness of flowers; on the corner of a damp napkin, on the other hand—an inspiration that had occurred to the aunt—the strange color was observed; the unfortunate child had imagined smearing her face with coral toothpaste, *to make herself prettier!*

But it was above all at the charity ball to which Lucile employed cunning to have herself taken—by means of God knows what cajolery—that Mademoiselle Cunégonde was edified on the subject of her niece.

Vanity, vanity, coquetry and vanity! That was what the little head was replete with.

The admiring gazes of men—an insult that Mademoiselle Cunégonde had always avoided—did not seem to offend Mademoiselle Lucile at all; she even provoked them by a fashion of having eyes more brilliant and cheeks more delicately rosy that was fitting for a truly modest person.

The aunt did not wait any longer to embark upon a salutary speech.

"My dear Lucile, I presume that you have retained a profound regret for the convent, where you must certainly have spent the happiest and holiest hours of your existence. I imagine that the contrast of the profane life into which you have entered, and of which you can obtain a troubling glimpse here, appears to you to be very afflicting."

"But no, Aunt, I was even beginning to be very bored at the convent, and if all of profane life is as gracious and gay as this hall full of pretty dresses and amiable messieurs, engaging music and colored lanterns, it must be exceedingly pleasant."

"Unfortunate child, who can have perverted your ideas in this fashion? What would the good sisters say on discovering such dispositions?"

"Oh, Aunt! As if anyone were going to tell the sisters what they think? Pupils write little letters to one another during class while appearing to do their assignments, and then, they talk in the dormitory while only paying attention to not waking up the supervisor."

"Monsieur l'Abbé, when he hears you confess, must be terrified to see such young souls already spoiled."

"Oh, Monsieur l'Abbé!"—here Lucile laughed madly and became pinker. "All the demoiselles were in love with Monsieur l'Abbé."

"What sacrilege! And do you dare to tell me than you . . ."

"Of course, I was in love with him, like all the others, but now I see that I was wrong."

"Thank Heaven, my poor child, that you repent of having allowed the purity of your soul to be tarnished by aberrations evidently provoked by the demon."

"No, Aunt, but I perceive that Monsieur l'Abbé was old and ugly. I see elegant young men here who please me far more. By the way, Aunt, why aren't you married? Weren't you pretty when you were young?"

"You should know, Mademoiselle, that that frivolous question has never preoccupied me; know, furthermore, that one doesn't question people like that; it's very inappropriate."

The next day, Mademoiselle Lucile returned to the paternal abode, and Aunt Cunégonde opened a certain drawer calmly and crossed the name of her niece out of her testament, in order to replace it with that of her nephew, Albert, Lucile's brother, who had left her the memory of a rather edifying first communion.

After that the old demoiselle resumed the course of her semi-cloistered life, receiving priests twice a week who came to dip fine cakes and blessed words in excellent tea.

✳

A year later, Aunt Cunégonde opened a letter:

> *My dear sister, there is good news and bad news. The good first: Lucile is married. She has found a superb party, Prince de ***, which is to say fortune, birth and a charming man.*
>
> *She has already been a princess for a fortnight, and it is surprising to see how that foolish girl has suddenly become a true wife of a grand seigneur, which she ought to be: energetic, intelligent and worthy in the governance of her household.*
>
> *The prince will live for a part of the year in his lands, and she is a little sovereign, very capable of reigning wherever he takes her.*
>
> *But if Lucile gives me contentment, it is not the same with her brother Albert.*

*He is leading an unqualifiable life, about
which it is very difficult for me to talk to you,
my dear sister, who are a saint, and which
threatens quite simply to ruin us . . .*

After reading that letter, Aunt Cunégonde remained
perplexed.

To have disinherited Lucile was no great inconvenience, since Lucile was a princess and rich, but to leave her fortune to that miscreant Albert became inadmissible. There remained their mother, who would doubtless be ruined, but was she not capable of weakness toward that Albert, who had gone astray in such bad ways?

At that moment, Monsieur l'Abbé arrived, very conveniently, to put an end to those uncertainties. The old lady made him the confidence of her scruples, and over afternoon tea the conversation revolved around the share of responsibility incumbent on those who, by virtue of a criminal indulgence, confide to frivolous hands that great weapon, wealth.

That evening, Mademoiselle de Brany opened her testament again, and, with a stroke of the pen, left her fortune to the reverend fathers.

And Lucile, who, that same evening, was leaning coquettishly on her elbow on the pillow, told her husband, among her childhood memories, about her sojourn with her aunt, having no suspicion that her mischief had cost her a million and a half.

POVERTY
A Legend
(*La Fronde*, 11 August 1899)

TWO brothers, Pavel and Yann, received the same heritage after the death of their father, an old peasant.

It was beautiful black and fecund land, where good Lithuanian wheat extended, undulating under delicate breezes, seeming to flow like a vast river of golden milk.

And rich herds of cows giving milk as white as the first snow, and sheep clad in nacreous curly wool, all of which, every spring, added dainty shiny ducats to those that had already been dormant for a long time in coffers.

Pavel, the elder, had taken for a wife a rich country-woman of the region.

Yann had married a poor girl whom he had loved since their childhood, and he was soon able to see around him living reminders of those charming years in the fine children that his wife gave him.

Pavel did not know that joy, but he consoled himself in seeing his wealth increased by his wife's dowry.

Thus, the two couples were living happily, each in its own manner, when calamities of all sorts began to strike Yann, more harshly with every season.

The beautiful cows with the tender eyes died one by one. They lay down sadly in fresh litter, and the naïve tears of Yann's daughters, their little friends, and their desperate prayers, were impotent to raise the docile muzzles that had once come in search, politely, in the hands of the young guardians, of a little grass picked when the flowers of the fields were still laughing.

Then the fields themselves became ill and languishing, like the animals.

The harvests were disastrous, and the sheep perished of hunger in meager and bare pastures.

And the shiny ducats fled like bees mad with fear from a burning hive.

Fire, the red enemy, devoured the buildings, which it was necessary to reconstruct with the last savings, and Yann found himself poor, after having been happy and rich.

Pavel avoided him, fearful of having to help a numerous family, or perhaps simply repelled by the misfortune that renders odious, as if soiled by a sinister leprosy, the vanquished of life.

Yann supported his disappointments proudly, without thinking any longer about his elder brother, but one day, poverty stung him too cruelly in his wife and family, crying famine, and he resolved to go and beg his brother for help.

Pavel was feasting like the brother of Lazarus, and the mere sight of Yann importuned him like the very spectacle of misfortune, and also like a secret remorse. Puhary eau-de-vie had warmed the heads of his guests, who started mocking their host for his calamitous family.

That finished exasperating Pavel, who ordered his servants to throw Yann out, after having thrown him, derisively, an immense ox-bone, the meat of which had sated the feasters.

Yann went away, mortally sick at heart, with the bone, which he had picked up mechanically, already doubled over by poverty, with the attitude of a starving dog.

Having returned home, he collapsed on a stool by the stove, the tall and broad stove, on which he had gone to sleep for such quiet hours in the happy times of old, in the good warmth of the enameled bricks.

Lugubrious reflections absorbed the poor fellow, and he sobbed, with his head in his hands.

Better to finish immediately with such a frightful existence, he thought, and his eyes sought some murderous implement. But only a long splinter of wood was within arms' reach, and he calculated the terrible time that an agony would last with that splinter stuck in his temple.

An insupportable dolor caused by hunger suddenly caused him to look at the bone, which he had thrown angrily into the isba.

Perhaps there's a little marrow left inside, the poor fellow thought, and, having picked up his brother's offering, he commenced to dig into it with the wooden splinter.

While Yann was savoring that pitiful meal, he saw a person descending from above the stove, stranger than any created being.

Her thinness surpassed the invention of the worst nightmares, and her jaws were clicking noisily with hunger and cold, grimacing a rictus of funereal mockery.

"Give me a little of what there is in that bone," the consternating visitor said to Yann, drawing closer. "I'm very hungry."

"Who are you, then, by God's holy angels?" howled the bewildered man.

"I'm your Poverty,"[1] replied the Specter. "It's me who has accompanied you faithfully for so many years, without ever being far away from you, and you owe it to me, for the trouble, to share your dinner with me."

"Gladly," said Yann, who had an idea. "Take what you wish for yourself."

Poverty stuck her whole head into the bone, but no great pittance remained there, and she was obliged to enter half her body thereinto. Then, in order to search harder, she disappeared into it completely.

Then, with the wooden splinter, Yann nailed her into the bone and went to drown his Poverty, from whom he was finally liberated, in the pond.

As he returned toward the house, his heart comforted with hope, he saw his wife running toward him joyfully.

On going to search for a few forgotten apples she had discovered a pot full of gold.

Yann redeemed his lands and his livestock, and everything succeeded for him from that day on in such a

---

1 Although the straightforward translation of *la Misère* as Poverty works very adequately within the context of the story, it is worth noting that the French term has other meanings, one of which is "Nothing," as in certain games of whist.

marvelous fashion that he became richer than ever, and much richer than his brother.

But Pavel was troubled by such sudden fortune.

"Yann has surely discovered some magical charm to enrich himself, some miraculous formula," he ruminated, every night, for sleep had deserted his anxious bed, "and it would be justice if he let me know it. Am I not his brother?"

And he decided one day to go and visit him. On the journey, all the way through Yann's property, Pavel's eyes were dazzled and his heart clawed by envy on seeing the surprising abundance flourishing in his younger brother's lands.

The wheat extended infinitely like a vast river of gilded honey undulating in the gentle breeze, and in the pastures, an entire placid population of brown cows was wandering, indolent and contented, browsing the opulent green grass with distracted mouths.

Yann received his elder brother cordially, having forgotten the past insults in his rediscovered happiness, and told him his astonishing story.

But Pavel, bitten by jealousy, was not disarmed by his younger brother's generosity.

Disappointed by not taking away the expected formula for enriching himself in his turn, he conceived the evil design of releasing on his brother the poverty captive at the bottom of the pond.

He went, therefore, to fish her out one night, not without difficulty, and released her from her prison.

But as soon as she was free, the Poverty leapt on to Pavel's shoulders and said to him:

"Thank you, thank you very much, for having liberated me. I shall never quit you, my brave benefactor, and I shall follow you faithfully everywhere, as I followed your brother."

The Poverty kept her word and no longer quit Pavel, whose ruin was accomplished in a few years.

Yann helped him until he died, after which the Poverty, deprived of her commensal, went to sit down on other shoulders.

And it is a great pity that she was not left drowned in the pond forever.

Perhaps, after all, the poverty of some is only made by the wickedness of others.

COMRADES
(*La Fronde*, 29 September 1899)

"LINETTE, Linette, how pretty you are today!"

"You're forgetting yourself, my dear."

"Pardon, Madame, I did, indeed, lose sight of our new conventions; we are at present two good comrades, nothing more."

"And how genteel that is, and how banal it is not, after having been . . ."

"After having been tender lovers."

"Tender! If you think that you've always been tender, with your absurd scenes . . ."

"And how delighted I am, fundamentally, that you're no longer my mistress. You'll never know how much you made me suffer with your coquetries."

"I only possess joy in thinking that there is in the world an amiable and witty fellow to whom I can show that I appreciate him without being exposed to him paying court to me."

"I shall be the only man in the world who has such a pretty comrade, with beautiful dresses incrusted with valenciennes, like this one, for example."

"We had an excellent idea there."

"An excellent idea."

"We'll tell one another everything, won't we?"

"Yes, everything."

"In any case, there won't be any reason for us to hide anything whatsoever from one another . . ."

"Where would good comradeship be without that frankness?"

"I ask myself that."

"On the contrary, you'll give me advice."

"Precious advice."

"Only a woman can see clearly into the games of other women, isn't that so?"

"Certainly. And you'll give me esthetic advice."

"With pleasure."

"Men know better than we do the adornment that renders us irresistible in their eyes."

This dialogue is bringing together in the Pavillon d'Armenonville, after a week of passionate agony, two beings who had adored one another madly for a year and whom a quarrel envenomed by friends—who does not have friends, alas?—had torn apart violently.

At present, through the vain noise of their words, they are savoring a paradisal felicity merely by sitting at the same table, being able to meet one another's gaze, having finished with the tortures of absence. "Absence is the greatest of woes." They are, in any case, getting a taste for this sport of camaraderie. Linette has never been so amused.

✳

Their rendezvous had sometimes taken place in artistic cabarets.

On those evenings, the reflections exchanged on the ridiculous singer clad in romantic velvet, and the mundane actress with the falsetto voice, penetrated them with intoxication, on condition that it was her who pulled the singer to pieces and him who denigrated the actress.

They went to the theater together, or to the country, and often an identical thought made them speak in chorus. Then there was joy and childish laughter.

Thus, they contented themselves with the small change of ideal possession, while awaiting something better.

Suddenly, they perceived that they were irremediably walled up in an attitude, and that neither of them wanted to be the first to depart from it, at any price.

Now, when they accompanied one another to the door, a casual handshake terminated the conversation, but the good comrade perished at the idea of the husband up above.

She, utterly anguished, searched the features of the ex-lover in every new encounter for the familiar traces of an amorous watchfulness,

Finally, exceeded by that constraint, he resolved to jump in with both feet.

That day, the two comrades were sitting on the terrace of the Ambassadors, and while the concert reached them in fragments of voices, damaged but full of implications, Linette exhumed an old grievance

"Once, didn't an ex-lover of mine whom you know very well squeeze my arm under the influence of I know not what hallucination . . . ?"

"It was that fat Yankee sitting next to us at the Circus, who was making eyes at you, without appearing to inconvenience you."

"In sum, you dared to squeeze my arm so brutally that the next day, there was a blue bracelet where your fingers had been."

"It was very pretty."

"Thank you. Fortunately, it's ancient history, and nothing similar can occur between us."

"That's true."

"Admire, then, how much better it is simply to be good comrades. Between lovers, one even ends up forgetting that one has been well brought up."

"Indeed. By the way, as we can tell one another everything, I'll tell you about a piquant adventure that happened to your servant no later than yesterday."

"Oh, yes, tell me that. Is it very funny?"

"To tell the truth, it loses much of its savor in being narrated, but for my part, I wasn't bored for a minute between midnight and two o'clock."

"Midnight and two o'clock?"

"Yes after having quit you."

"I thought you were going home to sleep?"

"Me too."

"So?" Here Linette's voice was slightly strangled, as if the young woman were swallowing through the jaws of a crocodile.

"So?" she repeated, while her partner looked at her.

"So, when I went home I found a woman lying in my bed."

"Very odd. And then?"

"She was a young provincial, a flirt of two years before, whom I'd forgotten hermetically. But for her the adventurette had remained an actuality. She called it giving her Parisian lover a surprise."

"And you found that quite natural, did you?"

"Well, if I had found the Eiffel Tower in the same place, limply extended, it wouldn't have seemed more extraordinary to me."

"You're doubtless going to see her again?"

By way of response he consulted his watch and made as if to summon the waiter.

"Between good comrades, one ought not to be embarrassed. I'll ask your permission to take you home a little earlier."

But he had not finished speaking when a resounding slap fell upon his cheek.

"You shan't go, wretch, monster, assassin!" cried the exquisite comrade, in tears, suddenly forgetting her good education and the pacific requirements of simple camaraderie, departing from them in a singular fashion.

And while an assembly commenced before the terrace, the couple reconciled in the jolting refuge of a cab, drowned in tears and kisses, pronouncing immortal words.

"Then the provincial woman was a trick?"

"Yes, Linette, a dirty trick."

"And . . . and you regret having tricked me so cruelly?"

"Not the shadow of a regret, Linette, my love; I was so unhappy being your comrade."

THE LITTLE FAY OF THE WOODS
(*La Fronde*, 8 December 1899)

NOW that December is here, with its damp cold, its dramatic winds, its pale suns sinking into hasty dusks it is particularly sweet to remember episodes of the cheerful season, to respire the dried flowers of memory, so close and already so far away, like all our memories, "fallen behind the times," according to the expression of the admirable Dickens.

We are sitting on the edge of a little path that passes through the wood.

The sun is rude, an August sun exasperated by the imminent autumn, going all in with an exalted flame, like someone who senses that he is growing old.

So, without even having the courage to penetrate under the trees, we content ourselves with that commencement of shadow.

And now on the path, we see something rolling toward us that resembles a powder puff, made of the down of an immaculate swan.

Momentarily, it made a bound and fell into the midst of the bushes, which then rendered the sound of a downpour.

It was a very small white cat.

The frequentation of humans had long ago impelled my love of animals as far as delirium.

Immediately, my hands were magnetized by the soft fur, desirous of contact with the thin perfect forms of suppleness and grace.

But we take a walk. The little devil is sometimes here, sometimes there. Suddenly, there it goes, climbing to the top of a tree trunk, from which it allows itself to fall like a fruit.

As if the tree were a white cattery.

However—attracted, it seems, by my wish—it approaches in little bounds and, an unexpected favor, installs itself on my knees with an amiable purr.

It creates a responsibility of souls, a young cat asleep on your dress.

It is all confident innocence, it is polite childhood, which is lavished in a thousand exuberant turns, and which repairs in sleep at the sound of the threaded distaff.

Naturally, I am no more able to move than a pebble, but our sleeper wakes up and I experience the need to take a few steps into the wood.

So here we are in the wood, walking, followed or preceded by the dazzling little animal that has taken us in amity.

At times it is like a will-o'-the-wisp fluttering above the grass; or, the rapid glide of its white coat streams as if silvered by the moon.

Sometimes, it is a little fay, gravely meditating, sitting on its backside in the midst of the grass.

Suddenly, an idea!

Eat the grass.

And now the cat is tearing up with its little carnivorous teeth, still innocent of any crime, thin strips of couch grass.

Then, again, a pensive pose in the green expanse; the impression of saying:

"I'll never eat all that.

"Aha! There's a butterfly. I must catch that, or I may not be worthy to be called a tomcat."

The light and nimble little beast stands up on two feet and dances like Mademoiselle Otero.[1]

But the ironic butterfly shrugs its wings, which make it inaccessible, and draws away without even hurrying.

At present, under a sunbeam that filters through the branches, our imp—which ought to be a cat—plays the odalisque, lying on his back, paws limply abandoned, tail trailing.

Now he can no longer be seen; he has disappeared.

"Puss! Puss!"

He reappears, gay and malicious, arriving at a little gallop. In the clearing we have reached, a small lump of rock emerges above a dried-up stream; he climbs to the summit and extends himself in the hieratic pose of a white stone sphinx.

---

1 Caroline Otero (1868-1965), known as "la belle Otero," was at the height of her fame in 1899, more so for her lovers—who allegedly included the crowned heads of Germany, England, Spain, Serbia and Monaco, plus a handful of Grand Dukes—than her dancing.

"We'll keep this little cat, he's a darling," I say, "and he's doubtless abandoned."

And we go back toward Gros Rouvres with the pretty animal, which follows us.

"Ah! He'd gone with you," says a farmer as we emerge from the wood, while his daughter avidly picks up the little white thing and hugs it in her arms.

"He's made us search for him everywhere, the little rogue."

We go back a little melancholy, thinking about the good she-cat as black as the devil, left in Paris in what the English call "the family way."

What if she were to surprise us by giving birth to an all-white kitten like that one?

The spirit of Edgar Poe brushes us. We imagine the omnipotent influence of human dreams acting deep in the entrails of a creature who loves you and wants to grant your wishes.

At present the little wood must be somber and morose.

My horizon is limited by curtains with attenuated hues in the bay window with colored glass.

The black she-cat has brought four children of the feline race into the world.

Not one of them is white.

But they are very pretty all the same: gray and marked like little jaguars, and for want of tree trunks, they climb the curtains.

DECEMBER
(*La Fronde*, 22 December 1899)

OLD Père Morin, very sprightly and vigorous in spite of his seventy years, goes home after a frigid morning in December spent supervising the laboring of his fields.

It is time for the postman's round and the rich peasant keeps up a rapid pace, in spite of the pinch of the ice. He is impatient to see the postman's braided cap and sack.

For no doubt, as Christmas is approaching, he will receive a letter from his son in Paris, his handsome Louis, a true monsieur, finishing his studies in pharmacy.

Ah! He has just appeared at the bend in the road, with his red collar turned down over his smock and his message-bearer's gaiters.

It is a whole stack of papers that he hands to Père Morin, and after a glass of white wine he sets forth again.

No letter from the lad, that's visible at the first glance; now, installed at the dining table Père Morin looks through the other envelopes rather mechanically, without interest.

A fine prospectus full of pictures attracts his attention, though.

It is in the avalanche of catalogues launched in towns and rural areas as the season of gifts approaches, that of a fashionable silversmith, Toc & Co.

Scandalized, the peasant reads:

Fruit bowl, twenty-centimeters, 75 francs.

"Wow! One could have a lot of fruit for that price—whole apple trees, not to mention duchesse pear trees."

Cream jug, two cups: 120 francs.

"Damn! For the price of the pair one could have a cow!"

Vegetable bowl, twenty-two centimeters, 80 francs.

"Good God, I'd rather eat out of the pigs' trough than serve myself from such dear trinkets."

Bread basket, 78 francs.

"Well, you could have a lot of bread for that price! Enough to mop up the soup in a whole arrondissement."

Water-jug with ice tube, 120 francs.

"Sacred thunder! I'd prefer a hundred and twenty francs' worth of good wine passing straight from the cellar to my own tube!"

At the same moment the Morin son, who has missed his morning lecture, having come home rather late the night before, is sitting down at table with Mademoiselle d'Arsouille, facing that beautiful person, who, before tucking into the radishes, is nonchalantly opening her mail, scattered among the hors-d'oeuvres.

That voluminous correspondence is composed, naturally, of numerous prospectuses and catalogues.

In spite of the early hour, Mademoiselle d'Arsouille's
eyes are already underlined with blue pencil, and an
abundant "java" is paling her face, which is beginning to
thicken at the approach of forty.

Suddenly, the reader becomes more especially interested by the examination of a catalogue.

It is that of Toc & Co. the fashionable silversmith.

"Look, darling, these are just what we lack for our
midnight feast, which ought to be ultra-chic:

"Water-jug with ice tube, fruit bowl, cream pot, and
all that isn't even very dear, for the latest thing.

"At the same time we can get this bonbon service:
fondant shovel, marron-glace tongs, candied fruit fork."

"Is that really indispensable?" hazards the Morin son.

"Is it indispensable? Without a doubt. Otherwise,
we'd look ridiculous before our guests."

Young Morin makes a slight instinctive grimace,
which makes him resemble momentarily Père Morin,
out there, swearing at the costly and useless trinkets—
but Mademoiselle d'Arsouille knows a fashion of looking at her lover, which has something of the siren and
something of the schoolmistress, which is completely
intimidating and irresistible.

So, at the moment when the maid brings the cutlets,
it is agreed that after lunch, they will take a cab to go to
the Toc & Co. store, to choose everything necessary to
ornament the table of the midnight feast.

FOR THE LOVE OF HEAVEN
(*La Fronde*, 26 January 1900)

MANETTE is no longer a child.
    Her fifteenth year has just sounded.
To the little bells of imminent lilies of the valley.

Meanwhile, she is insouciant and cheerful, like an oriole at the first flap of its wings outside the nest.

Everything is a marvel in that freshly-hatched spring.

The frost of flowers of the braches of the cherry-trees, the light song of the stream.

The new-born lawns where flocks are grazing.

The woodland pathways that are naves when the organ of spring breezes is singing.

And above all the beautiful pure blue sky, like a great open eye.

Toward evening, the sky becomes greener.
    A little like the new-born lawns.
    And the white clouds graze there like free flocks.

So Manette, all day long, and until dusk, is as cheerful as the birds.

Sometimes she tries to imitate their songs, sometimes she laughs with them.

And why all that delight, why does Manette laugh like the oriole?

Like him, without knowing why: for nothing, for the love of spring.

For the love of Heaven.

It is not the first time that the young lord of the château has come to talk to Manette in a coaxing voice.

She listens without displeasure and looks at his handsome face as she looks around at the graces of spring.

What pride there is in learning that one is beautiful from such a knowledgeable young man.

For in the village it is said that the young lord—being the younger brother—will soon be an abbé, and later, a bishop or perhaps a cardinal.

He does not appear to be one for the moment.

Mischievously, he is able to retain the hands of the fearful Manette, who tries to flee like a captured oriole.

At other times, they laugh, both leaning over the song of the stream.

But one day, Manette understands that those games are full of perils, that all her soul of a little shepherdess is going to be stolen by the young lord of the château.

278

She knows already that if he does not take pity on her, she will not be able to defend herself.

"Oh Monsieur, leave me be, leave me be, for the love of Heaven."

✳

It is too late.

If the young lord grants Manette's wish, Manette will die of it.

So they abandon themselves radiantly, powerfully, as if they were the first born on the earth to the happiness of amour.

The entire landscape around them has become a Paradise.

The woodland pathways are naves in which the spring breezes sing their hymen.

The voice of the nests is an echo of their kisses.

And their hearts bloom, as ardent as the poppies in the meadows.

✳

Until the day when the friend says to Manette:

"Alas. Manette, the hour of adieux has come.

"I must return this heart that was so completely yours to the One who reclaims it as his promised due.

"I must make myself a priest."

And Manette senses her soul tearing apart within her, as if traversed by a sharp blade.

She will not survive that blow.

She is so sure of it that it consoles her.

But in order not to sadden her dear lord at that supreme moment, she simply says:

"Since that is your destiny, Monseigneur, since you are promised to the Master of Heaven, go to your destiny.

"I renounce you, for love of you, and for the love of Heaven."

IN THE CLEARING
(*La Fronde*, 26 January 1900)

IN a clearing in the wood, Tancred and Tristan, after a combat, have fallen, mortally wounded.

Lady Isabeau was the object of their quarrel, for they both loved her.

They were two proud companions in battle, with noble hearts and loyal swords.

Tancred thinks: *Tristan, one day, for my defense, received a master thrust of a lance.*

And Tristan remembers: *To save my life, Tancrede was stricken by a Saracen pike.*

"Adieu, dear brother," they say, in unison, sensing death coming.

"Adieu, and may Christ pardon us!"

Meanwhile, the woman they love—to the point of this barbaric death—Lady Isabeau, is simpering and purring with her cithara-master.

TROUPE ON TOUR
(*La Fronde*, 2 March 1900)

THE beautiful clear night prolonged the day over the sleeping countryside, and we traversed the Loiret, the Nivernais and the commencement of the Auvergne without losing any of the enchantment of the landscapes framed in the window of the carriage.

After having ballasted herself with roast beef confected by some vigilant aunt, the lead singer is lying theatrically on a sofa, her hair powdered, with a white mantilla, evoking a cheapjack Carmen, knees buried in a goatskin, aiming for regal effect.

Soon, however, the rocking of the train lulls her into a slumber revelatory of vulgarity. The lips, winnowed by the permanent general rehearsal of an enchanting smile, relax into the negligence of a pout, the undersides of the eyes admit their wear and tear.

The juvenile lead, decked out in a hideous sportsman's cap is cuddling a malodorous inflated rubber pillow. The pianist and stage manager was sinking his fatigue is a brightly-colored muffler, and he was no more able to admire the beauty of the night than me and the fine J., the composer of wild and new melodies that were once so celebrated, and who then required of his beautiful baritone voice the wherewithal to prevent the future dear master from dying of hunger.

Against the distant sky the trees stood out with a refined measure of clarity and vaporousness.

In the plains and on the hills, the steeples and the hamlets were immaculate Paros marble, the tree trunks polished silver and the labored soil had tints of pink ivory.

Then valleys filled with light resembled immense bowls filled with milk.

Again, cities of marble surged forth, which were nothing but humble villages magnified by the prestigious star.

A grunt like an angry sow.

That was Romeo, Paolo, Hamlet and the King of Rome, who, synthesized in the juvenile lead, had abandoned himself, snoring, to the joys of slumber.

Without allowing ourselves to be discouraged by those sorry examples, we ended up becoming drowsy ourselves, and I like to suppose that we had a more decorative slumber.

The dawn was saluted by all of our admiration as artistes, and all our joy in seeing that nightmarish night end, in which somnolence was interrupted at regular intervals by the maneuvers of human devils who let in blasts of icy air through noisily opened doors in order to change the foot-warmers in the compartment.

The train is now rolling through the rocky hills of the Allier, and curiously enough, it is in the Midi, the empire of the sun, that we find long-forgotten snowy landscapes again.

In the distance, the Cévennes raise their peaks like the white heads of grandfathers.

Closer, amid the rocks and the somber brushwood, large masses of snow have collapsed like flocks of dying ibis.

On the mountainsides, more snow, broken up by broom and dry heather, the shadow of which, projected by the already-burning sun, takes on the suave tones of heliotropes and Parma violets, which might have been strewn there in bunches.

The absurd and perverse evocation of a Spring asleep in the bosom of Winter, like a young woman in the arms of an aged husband.

But here is a consternating marvel, the valley of the Tarn.

From my sojourns in mountainous countries I have carried away an impression of the hostility of the décor, bruising for an inhabitant of the plain, oppressive for eyes amorous of vast horizons, rancorous because of those abruptly-devoured suns fallen behind the mountain when, in the lowlands or shallow valleys one can see the pompous spectacle of its slow setting.

But here, while the train runs, no comparison can be presented to the mind.

One is outside the world, time and space.

The very sensation of being placed on a flat surface is abolished.

It is as if our eyes, after the heavy slumber of death, were opening to the light of another planet, and there, our new condition having endowed us with wings, it is permissible for us to soar in space.

Vast undulations of rocks, all in supple spirals, as if some ancient vanished ocean had rounded off the angles, alternate in serene harmony the contours of lines.

The open sea offers those effects.

But in plunging the gaze into the gorges in which a torrent sparkles, we understand above what abysses those noble summits loom, clad in suave tints infinitely degraded, which, after having exhausted all the memories of the most delightful flowers and the most precious crystals, diffuse in unknown, unnamable hues.

And occasionally, on a slope, a little country hangs, an imperceptible nest of poor human insects.

Nearer, granitic rocks scaled by rare bouquets of savage vegetation, which stain the stone, make it resemble a panther shin, and make one think of the ancient relationship of every created thing.

More rocks crowned with sumptuous and eccentric architectures, built by global cataclysms, sculpted by avalanches, on which human effort has modeled its effort.

Here are ineradicable fortresses with their crenellated surrounding walls, Roman cities and, under a flood of carmines and pale ochers, Indian pagodas and the temples of meditative Egypt in which the gods are seated forever.

The composer J., gripped by admiration, says to me:

"This is humiliating for humans, and reminds them how small a place they occupy in the universe."

I experience the need to contradict him, in these terms:

"You're mistaken, my friend. All this beauty, all this grandeur would be non-existent if they did not find, here facing them, the emotional heart of an artist, which reflects their glory in its admiration, which *observes* that beauty and that grandeur."

A PARTIAL LIST OF SNUGGLY BOOKS

G. ALBERT AURIER *Elsewhere and Other Stories*

S. HENRY BERTHOUD *Misanthropic Tales*

LÉON BLOY *The Desperate Man*

LÉON BLOY *The Tarantulas' Parlor and Other Unkind Tales*

ÉLÉMIR BOURGES *The Twilight of the Gods*

JAMES CHAMPAGNE *Harlem Smoke*

FÉLICIEN CHAMPSAUR *The Latin Orgy*

FÉLICIEN CHAMPSAUR
    The Emerald Princess and Other Decadent Fantasies

BRENDAN CONNELL *Clark*

BRENDAN CONNELL *Jottings from a Far Away Place*

BRENDAN CONNELL *Unofficial History of Pi Wei*

RAFAELA CONTRERAS *The Turquoise Ring and Other Stories*

ADOLFO COUVE *When I Think of My Missing Head*

QUENTIN S. CRISP *Aiaigasa*

QUENTIN S. CRISP *Graves*

LADY DILKE *The Outcast Spirit and Other Stories*

CATHERINE DOUSTEYSSIER-KHOZE *The Beauty of the Death Cap*

ÉDOUARD DUJARDIN *Hauntings*

BERIT ELLINGSEN *Now We Can See the Moon*

BERIT ELLINGSEN *Vessel and Solsvart*

ENRIQUE GÓMEZ CARRILLO *Sentimental Stories*

EDMOND AND JULES DE GONCOURT *Manette Salomon*

REMY DE GOURMONT *From a Faraway Land*

GUIDO GOZZANO *Alcina and Other Stories*

EDWARD HERON-ALLEN *The Complete Shorter Fiction*

RHYS HUGHES *Cloud Farming in Wales*

J.-K. HUYSMANS *Knapsacks*

COLIN INSOLE *Valerie and Other Stories*

JUSTIN ISIS *Pleasant Tales II*

JUSTIN ISIS AND DANIEL CORRICK (editors)
    Drowning in Beauty: The Neo-Decadent Anthology

FREDERICK ROLFE (Baron Corvo) *Amico di Sandro*

FREDERICK ROLFE (Baron Corvo)
An Ossuary of the North Lagoon and Other Stories

JASON ROLFE *An Archive of Human Nonsense*

BRIAN STABLEFORD (editor)
Decadence and Symbolism: A Showcase Anthology

BRIAN STABLEFORD (editor) *The Snuggly Satyricon*

BRIAN STABLEFORD *The Insubstantial Pageant*

BRIAN STABLEFORD *Spirits of the Vasty Deep*

BRIAN STABLEFORD *The Truths of Darkness*

COUNT ERIC STENBOCK *Love, Sleep & Dreams*

COUNT ERIC STENBOCK *Myrtle, Rue & Cypress*

COUNT ERIC STENBOCK *The Shadow of Death*

COUNT ERIC STENBOCK *Studies of Death*

MONTAGUE SUMMERS *The Bride of Christ and Other Fictions*

GILBERT-AUGUSTIN THIERRY *The Blonde Tress and The Mask*

GILBERT-AUGUSTIN THIERRY *Reincarnation and Redemption*

DOUGLAS THOMPSON *The Fallen West*

TOADHOUSE *Gone Fishing with Samy Rosenstock*

TOADHOUSE *Living and Dying in a Mind Field*

RUGGERO VASARI *Raun*

JANE DE LA VAUDÈRE *The Demi-Sexes and The Androgynes*

JANE DE LA VAUDÈRE *The Double Star and Other Occult Fantasies*

JANE DE LA VAUDÈRE *The Mystery of Kama and Brahma's Courtesans*

JANE DE LA VAUDÈRE *The Priestesses of Mylitta*

JANE DE LA VAUDÈRE *Syta's Harem and Pharaoh's Lover*

JANE DE LA VAUDÈRE *Three Flowers and The King of Siam's Amazon*

JANE DE LA VAUDÈRE *The Witch of Ecbatana and The Virgin of Israel*

AUGUSTE VILLIERS DE L'ISLE-ADAM *Isis*

RENÉE VIVIEN AND HÉLÈNE DE ZUYLEN DE NYEVELT
Faustina and Other Stories

RENÉE VIVIEN *Lilith's Legacy*

RENÉE VIVIEN *A Woman Appeared to Me*

KAREL VAN DE WOESTIJNE *The Dying Peasant*